# ERLE STANLEY GARDNER

- Cited by the *Guinness Book of World Records* as the #1 bestselling writer of all time!

- Author of more than 150 clever, authentic, and sophisticated mystery novels!

- Creator of the amazing Perry Mason, the savvy Della Street, and dynamite detective Paul Drake!

- **THE ONLY AUTHOR WHO OUT-SELLS AGATHA CHRISTIE, HAROLD ROBBINS, BARBARA CARTLAND, AND LOUIS L'AMOUR *COMBINED!***

Why?

Because he writes the best, most fascinating whodunits of all!

You'll want to read every one of them, from
**BALLANTINE BOOKS**

# The Case of the
# Bigamous Spouse

## Erle Stanley Gardner

BALLANTINE BOOKS • NEW YORK

# Foreword

For many years now I have been interested in telling the public about the importance of legal medicine.

Recently I have become interested in some of the Japanese doctors who have specialized in this field.

From time to time I have dedicated my books to leaders in the field of forensic medicine. I have watched the manner in which the real leaders in this field have weeded out the expert *witness* who was the bane of the profession years ago, and have developed the *expert* witness whose devotion is to truth, whose only loyalty is to scientific accuracy, whose sole objective is to assist justice by developing the true facts in the field of scientific research.

Few people realize the importance of what is being discovered in the field of blood and blood grouping.

Thanks to the dedicated work of the hematologists we are now able to bring the searchlight of scientific accuracy to bear upon many cases of disputed paternity. We are able to save many lives which would otherwise be lost.

Dr. Yokoyama tells me hematologists at present are able to classify approximately forty blood group systems, seventy blood group factors and more than 100,000,000,000 theoretically possible genotypes.

Constantly, day and night, these scientists are pushing back the frontiers of knowledge.

The Japanese scientist is peculiarly gifted in this field because he combines the patience of the Oriental with his inherent powers of observation, his passion for detail with the zealous devotion of a dedicated scientist.

I have recently come in contact with Dr. Mitsuo Yokoyama, who, while a relatively young man, has nevertheless achieved international recognition for his work in the field of hematology.

And because I would like to have my readers realize something of the vital importance of legal medicine and recognize the great strides which have been made by the Japanese medical profession in the field of research, I respectfully dedicate this book to my friend

MITSUO YOKOYAMA, M.D., Ph.D.

ERLE STANLEY GARDNER

# Cast of Characters

# Chapter 1

Della Street, Perry Mason's confidential secretary, had a mischievous twinkle in her eyes. Her right hand was held behind her back.

"Good morning, Mr. Mason," she said.

The lawyer looked up from his desk, caught the twinkle in her eyes, tilted back in his swivel chair and said, "What now?"

"I wanted some information."

"Shoot."

"Can you," she asked, "tell me the principle on which the telephone works, and how a voice can be transferred into electrical vibrations sent over a wire and then those vibrations again turned back into audible sounds so that the voice seems to come through the receiver?"

"Certainly," Mason said. "You simply drop a dime in the slot indicated for such purpose."

"Can you," Della Street asked, "tell me why it is that it is noon in New York when it is only nine o'clock in Los Angeles?"

"Of course," Mason said. "The people in New York get up three hours earlier."

"Try this one," she said. "Why is it that on a hot day in the California desert it is possible to look up at tall mountain ranges and observe that they are covered with snow?"

Mason's forehead began to show traces of a frown. "You're too big to spank," he said, "and too valuable to fire, but if you'll kindly tell me what's the idea . . ."

"You were complaining only a short time ago," she said,

1

"that the practice of law tends to become routine; that just as the newspapers feature murder, robbery and rape, day after day, the only difference being the names of the persons affected, the practice of law tends to become generalized according to pattern. Now, I thought I would convince you, Mr. Mason, that here we have something new."

"What," Mason asked, "is the relationship of the snow on the California mountains to something new in the law business?"

Della Street whipped her hand from behind her back and disclosed an elaborately printed brochure.

"On this page," she said, "are thirty-seven questions which your child may ask. Do you know the answers?"

She turned the page. "Here are fifteen physical phenomena which are often misunderstood, and here on the next page are fifty interesting facts which few people understand."

"I take it," Mason said, "that on the back page is a contract with a place for signature and a receipt for the down payment."

"Not a contract," she said, "a coupon, by which the person who signs it can receive detailed information about a booklet entitled, *Practical Physical Facts for Parents* and, imprinted on that is the name, *Gwynn Elston*, with an address and telephone number at which Miss Elston can be reached."

"And you think I should sign my name," Mason asked gravely, "so that I will be prepared to become a father?"

"That won't be necessary," Della Street said, "because Miss Elston is sitting in the outer office patiently waiting. She gave me this little brochure because it gives her name and address. I asked her if she had a card and this was all she had."

"Well," Mason said, "I'm afraid you're going to have to tell Miss Elston that after all I'm not interested in—Let's see."

2

Mason took the brochure and turned to some of the interesting questions. "Tell her I don't care a hang why it is that whales spout on coming to the surface. I don't care why certain animals hibernate, nor am I interested in why days are longer in the summer than in the winter. I feel that I can get along without knowing why water kept in a porous earthernware jug is cooler than water placed alongside it in a plain glass bottle."

"That," Della Street said, "is not the point. Miss Elston doesn't want to sell you a book, she wants to see if you can translate certain Chinese characters for her, and whether her crumpled piece of tissue contains strychnine."

"That's all?" Mason asked.

"It seems to be all at the moment," Della Street said, "although I dare say there are other things which will come up. She seems quite upset and rather excited. Despite the rain she looks as dry as a potato chip. She must have left a raincoat in the car. And she *does* have legs!"

"How old?" Mason asked.

"In her twenties," Della Street said. "And for your private and confidential information she's a dish! Nothing blatant or voluptuous, you understand, but plenty of this and that and these and those; large, expressive eyes and a voice which would be seductive if it weren't a little frightened."

"And here it was only an hour ago," Mason said, "I was complaining that our law practice was getting in a rut. By all means, Della, show Miss Elston in. And what about the crumpled tissue?"

"She has it in her purse."

"And wants to know if it contains strychnine?"

Della Street nodded.

"Why?"

"Someone tried to poison her."

"An irate wife, perhaps?"

"Apparently it was the husband of her best friend."

3

Perry Mason said seriously. "Do you suppose there is any chance on earth that this case is one-tenth as interesting as you're making it sound?"

"Somehow," Della Street said, "I have an idea it's even more interesting, although I admit I did try to doll it up a bit."

"Let's take a look at her," Mason said.

Della Street nodded and glided quietly through the door to the outer office.

# Chapter 2

Gwynn Elston acknowledged Della Street's introduction to the lawyer, seated herself, smoothed her skirt over her knees, made a token gesture of pulling down the hem, smiled at the lawyer and said, "Mr. Mason, in order to understand my problem you'll have to know something about how I work."

The lawyer nodded his head gravely.

"I have an assigned territory," she said, "for a series of books which are designed to give parents the answers to questions that children will want to know. The books are so cleverly arranged that there is really no age limit. Not only are the answers listed to questions which will be asked by the very young, but there is information which even the adult . . ."

She broke off with a quick laugh. "I'm sorry, Mr. Mason, but I've repeated this so many times that when I start on it I just can't seem to stop and condense. I'm giving you what is known in the trade as 'the canned approach'—anyway, you get the idea."

Mason said, "I am afraid, Miss Elston, I'm not in the market for—"

"Good heavens!" she said. "I'm not trying to sell *you*. I . . . I'm afraid I'm going to be mixed up in a murder."

"That," Mason said, "is different. Just what is your position going to be in the murder?"

She said, "I think I'm scheduled to be what you might call the *pièce de résistance*."

"Meaning the victim?"

She nodded.

"Go ahead," Mason said.

"I'm sorry to bother you with all this background, Mr. Mason, but you have to understand it because otherwise what I'm going to tell you will seem just too dreadfully absurd and you'll think I'm the victim of an overworked imagination."

The lawyer inclined his head in a wordless invitation to proceed.

"The parent company give us all sorts of sales helps, does advertising and secures lists of live prospects so that we don't have to waste our time in fruitless door-to-door canvassing. Those prospects are sent in at the rate of about ten a day. Sometimes they mail them in, sometimes they telephone them. We're supposed to make a schedule of ten new calls a day, in addition of follow-ups."

"What is a live prospect?" Mason asked.

"A family in the income group of six thousand a year on up, with two children or more, and usually parents who are rather young. They're more . . . well, more progressive."

Again Mason nodded.

"Nell Arlington is my closest friend," Gwynn Elston went on. "She married Felting Grimes and came to live here in the city. They have a very nice house. There is a spare room as well as a guesthouse. . . . I guess the spare room was originally intended as a servant's quarters. It has its own washbowl and toilet, but it also has a connection with the downstairs bath. Now, please bear with me, Mr. Mason, because all this is important."

Mason nodded.

"A year or so ago something happened in my life," Gwynn Elston said. "The rug was jerked out from under me. I was left emotionally stranded and financially broke. Nell insisted that I come to visit her for a few weeks until things straightened out.

"Nell is full of ideas and initiative and it was through her that I answered an ad and became a saleswoman for this book company, and I've been there ever since."

"How do you and Nell's husband get along?" Mason asked.

"That's the point, Mr. Mason. Of course, at first he tolerated me and then he began looking me over with a roving eye. You understand in the intimacy of a household that way there were lots of opportunities for him to see me . . . well, when I wasn't fully dressed."

"Did you help create those opportunities?" Mason asked.

"Lord, no!" she said, with feeling. "I detest the man."

"But you're leading up to something in your relationship?"

"Yes."

"What?"

"He made passes."

"So you wanted to leave?"

"Yes."

"And what happened?"

"Nell laughed at me. She said that she knew he'd make passes; that all men make passes at good-looking women; that she trusted me to be her friend and see that the 'No Trespassing' signs were put up in the proper places."

"And you did that?"

"I did that, perhaps too abruptly, and Felting Grimes had his little ego hurt and started sulking, and then started a series of little, petty persecutions designed to get rid of me."

"And now I take it," Mason said, "he's about to become successful and—"

"No, no, Mr. Mason! You couldn't ever guess this in a hundred years."

"Well," Mason said, "I haven't got a hundred years and

7

I have another appointment in thirty minutes, so you'd better tell me."

She said, "Felting Grimes is away from home a lot. He is some kind of a business sharpshooter. Nell had always been rather indefinite about what he does, and I think that's because he's never really told her. Anyhow, he travels a lot and makes investments, and always seems to have plenty of money, but as long as I've known them I've never been able to find out *exactly* what he does."

"You've asked him?"

"No, I've asked Nell."

"And what does Nell say?"

"Nell laughs and says she doesn't want to be bothered with business details, that when Felt comes home all he wants is feminine companionship, apple pie with lots of sugar and cinnamon, and a chance to be free of business worries."

"Your friend, Nell, sounds like quite a character," Mason said.

"She is. . . . Now, I think I've given you enough of a background so you can understand what I'm going to tell you.

"Yesterday the list of prospects that was sent to me included Frankline Gillett. . . . Do you know where the George Belding Baxter estate is, out near Vista del Mesa?"

"Generally," Mason said.

"Well, this is on Tribly Way, about a quarter of a mile beyond the Baxter estate. It's a new subdivision suburb."

"And you went to call on Frankline Gillett?" Mason asked.

"On Mrs. Gillett. We always try to work our schedule so that we have our first contact with the woman of the house and quite freqently we never see the man at all. You see, one of the requirements of our employment is that we have personality and . . . well, rather striking figures.

"Sometimes the woman of the house likes to have us

meet her husband when the transaction is ready to be closed, but generally the woman prefers to put the proposition up to her husband and then give us the answer the next day. In that way we never meet the husband."

"And the woman doesn't bring any new competition into the picture?" Mason asked.

Gwynn Elston laughed self-consciously. "Something like that," she said. "In fact, we're given instructions to dress a lot more demurely when we keep an evening appointment with the prospect when the husband is there. During the daytime we're supposed to dress, well, rather strikingly. It's the theory of the company that women are interested in talking with other women who have what the company refers to as vivid personalities, charm and nice legs. . . . Really, Mr. Mason, I'm letting my hair down with you, and I know how busy you are! You want me to come to the point and . . . well, here it is in a nutshell: Frankline Gillett is really Felting Grimes."

Mason raised his eyebrows. "Just how do you know?"

She said, "To begin with, when I called on Mrs. Gillett, right in the middle of my talk with her, the door opened and her son came running into the room."

"How old?" Mason asked.

"Seven."

"Go ahead," Mason said.

"That boy," she said, "was the absolute image of Felting Grimes. I was never so shocked in my life. I tried to talk and couldn't. I finally had the presence of mind to have a coughing fit."

"Many times," Mason said, "startling resemblances are coincidental."

Gwynn nodded, said, "I understand that, Mr. Mason. Believe me, I wouldn't be bothering you if I weren't . . . well, if I weren't certain and if it weren't for the fact that these other complications have taken place."

"All right," Mason said, "go on. Let's hear the rest of it."

"Well, I got over my fit of coughing and made quite a bit over Frankline, Junior and asked him questions. I asked him about his daddy, and asked him whether his daddy had been a soldier. You see, Felt—that is, Felting Grimes—had been in the Air Force and had served in Nationalist China, and sure enough, young Frankie Gillett told me his dad had been in the Air Force and had served in China. I asked him if he had a picture of his daddy and he went and got a picture and . . . well, it was a picture of Felting Grimes, all right, taken in China and— Well, then I guess I wasn't very tactful. I asked too many questions about his father, and Mrs. Gillett told Frankie to run along and play."

"And did you say anything to her that would let her know you had recognized the picture?" Mason asked.

"Lord no! I went right ahead and concentrated on my sales pitch and did a good job of it. She asked me to come back this evening . . . There were some Chinese characters shown on the hangar in the picture of his father that Frankie brought me, and I memorized the four biggest characters and then, later on, made a sketch of them. Here they are.

"Now, Felting Grimes was in the Air Force in China, and if you can have those Chineses characters translated, we can identify the air base—and that will give me enough proof so I can face Nell—if I have to."

"When was it you had the interview with Mrs. Gillett?" Mason asked.

"Yesterday—yesterday afternoon."

"And she wanted you to come back this evening because her husband was going to be home?"

"I don't know, Mr. Mason. She just asked me if I could come back tomorrow night at eight-thirty. That would be tonight."

"All right," Mason said, "now, what about the poison?"

She said, "I went back to Nell's house last night and right

away I could tell that Felting Grimes was suspicious. He asked me where I'd been; he asked me how business was, how many calls I'd made, and all about my prospects, and then he started asking me about names."

"But you didn't have to tell him that you'd been calling on the Gilletts," Mason said.

"That's just the point—I did, Mr. Mason. You see, sometimes the company writes in a list of prospects, sometimes it telephones them. I telephone Nell whenever I've finished the list I have, and if more have been mailed in, Nell reads them off to me. If the company telephones, Nell answers, and when she knows it's the representative of the company calling, and they ask for Gwynn Elston, Nell simply says, 'This is Miss Elston talking,' and then they will give her a list of prospects and Nell will write them down."

"And what happened this time?"

Gwynn Elston said, "She may have left the list hanging around where Felt could have seen it, so that he knew, or could have known, that I'd been out to call on the Gilletts.

"So you can see the spot I was in. If I lied to him and told him I hadn't been out there, then he'd know I was suspicious, so the only thing for me to do was to act just as though the name, Frankline Gillett, was just the same as any other prospect to me."

"And you did that?"

She nodded.

"Then what?"

"Well, everything was all right, but last night when we were having a nightcap and he'd mixed me a drink of my regular gin and tonic, it tasted so terribly bitter that I made an excuse to go to my room, and while I was there I dumped it down the washbowl, rinsed out the glass, filled it half full of plain water, and came back and drank it as though I were drinking the gin and tonic.

"Later on, when I went to bed, I kept thinking about it. I

went to the washbowl, moistened my finger, ran it along the side of the washbowl, and then put the finger to my mouth, and it was just as bitter as could be. So I took this piece of tissue and and cleaned the bowl out. I wanted to see if— well, if there was strychnine on it."

"And if it should turn out there is strychnine, then what?" Mason asked.

"Well, then I'd know that— Good heavens, Mr. Mason, you can see for yourself! The man is desperate. He simply couldn't afford to have Nell find out about his double life, and he'd kill me in a minute in order to keep from being discovered. There's something terribly sinister about Felting Grimes. Nell loves him, or at least thinks she does. Anyhow, she's happy. I guess they're perfectly adjusted sexually, and Nell is broad-minded and doesn't ask questions, isn't jealous, and doesn't have any of the . . . well, you know, the symptoms of frustration."

"Any children?" Mason asked.

"No children, but— In a situation of that sort, you can realize what would happen. Nell could completely ruin the man. In fact, if it came out . . . well, I guess it means a prison sentence, doesn't it?"

"Which one would have been wife number one, and which one the bigamous spouse?" Mason asked.

"I don't know."

"But you know that young Frankline Gillett, or Frankie, as they call him, is seven years old and—"

"And that doesn't mean a thing, Mr. Mason. I think that's one of the reasons Mrs. Gillett sent him out of the room when I got to asking questions. You know . . . they could have had an affair and Frankie could have . . . well, you know, been illegitimate. And then afterwards she could have persuaded Felting to marry her. . . . Heavens, it's all too mixed up for me!"

"Well," Mason said, "under the circumstances we'd

better get the thing straightened out. You hadn't better go back to your room until—"

"Oh, but I have to, Mr. Mason. Otherwise, Nell would have seventeen fits. She'd be calling the police and— No, that's all right. Felting Grimes left this morning on one of his business trips. He's not going to be back for a week. Nell and I have the house all to ourselves."

"Then tonight," Mason said, "Frankline Gillett may return from one of *his* business trips."

She nodded.

"You intend to go out there?" Mason asked.

"Mr. Mason, I have to. I have to go through with it and— Don't you see, it's my only chance. If I can carry on just as though I didn't suspect a thing, then I'll get a sort of reprieve."

"You don't think you'll meet the husband tonight?"

"Oh, no. If he comes home and Mrs. Gillett tells him that I'm to call, he'll make some excuse to be out. He certainly isn't going to let me face him and recognize him—not unless he's prepared to kill me right there."

"He could hardly do that," Mason said.

"That's the way I feel about it, Mr. Mason. I don't think there's any chance that *he'll* be there. And if I'm a good enough actress to carry the whole thing off as just another assignment, another prospect that didn't come through . . . well, then, *I'll* be in the clear."

"But you wouldn't want to let Nell go on living the way she is."

"Heavens, no! And I wouldn't want to be at her house too long after Felting Grimes comes back. Unless, of course, it's all my imagination about the strychnine."

"As soon as you're sure, you're going to tell Nell?"

"Yes, but I have to be absolutely, positively certain, Mr. Mason."

The lawyer nodded.

"Then," Gwynn Elston went on thoughtfully, "I've

13

simply got to tell Nell, but heaven knows what she'll do. She's perfectly capable of keeping her mouth and staying right on living with him as his part-time wife. Mrs. Gillett is the one that would raise the roof."

"You think she would?"

"I feel sure she would. She's one of those thin-lipped, determined people who are nice and polite in a formal, cold sort of way but . . . well, she isn't vital like Nell is. Nell is broad-minded and easygoing, and she has ideas. She says that if a woman can't keep her husband satisfied, some other woman is going to do it."

"And Mrs. Gillett isn't that type at all?"

"Not at all," Gwynn said, shaking her head vehemently. "Believe me, after you've punched as many doorbells as I have, you can tell all about them . . . size them up, I mean."

"All right," Mason said, "if you want to go out there tonight, go ahead, but remember this: Don't eat anything, don't drink anything while you're in that house. If the husband is home, and it should turn out to be Felting Grimes, don't make any scene, don't make any accusation, don't say anything that would cause Mrs. Gillett to know that she is a bigamous wife. When she introduces you to her husband, don't let on that you've ever seen him before. However, here's one of my cards. You hand him that card and say, 'Do you know Perry Mason, the lawyer? I was talking with him this morning and he thinks he knows you. He said that it might be a good thing for you to get in touch with him.'"

"Do you think he'd do that?" she asked.

"He might, or he might not," Mason said, "but it would at least let him know that you'd told me everything and that nothing would be gained by trying to silence you."

"Oh, yes, I see. . . . It all sounds so terribly theatrical and impossible when you tell about it in the security of a lawyer's office, with lawbooks and—" She smiled at Della

Street—"a sympathetic secretary, and all the things that go with the administration of justice. I feel like pinching myself to see if it isn't a dream, and then I feel like a fool for bothering you with it."

"Not at all," Mason said. "You'd be surprised at how many unconventional stories have been told within the four walls of this office. Some of them sound completely bizarre. . . . You're sure that you want to go out there tonight?"

"Oh, yes, I have to, Mr. Mason. Otherwise, Felting Grimes would know that I'd smelled a rat. No, I'm satisfied I'm perfectly safe now, at least until Felting Grimes gets back home. And I'm safe then *if* I can play my cards right tonight. However, it's not *my* safety I'm thinking of. I'm Nell's friend and . . . well, whatever Nell wants to do is up to her, but she has to know the facts. I just feel two-faced living there with her and not telling her—holding out on her."

"You've been very close?"

"Oh, yes. We roomed together and we used to tell each other everything; all about the different boys who made passes."

"And those who didn't?" Mason asked.

She laughed throatily. "There weren't any."

"All right," Mason told her, "leave your address with Della Street, your telephone number, and you have my card. And in case you should want to call me this evening, here's the number of the Drake Detective Agency. That's a detective agency on the same floor of this building. Paul Drake does all my investigative work. They're open twenty-four hours a day. I'll leave word that if you should call tonight they're to relay the call through to me."

"You're very kind," she said. "About . . . about a retainer."

Mason nodded toward the brief case she was carrying. "How much money do you make out of this?" he asked.

"Pretty good money sometimes. I average six or seven hundred dollars a month. I'm paying off some old debts—I really got hit quite a financial wallop—I have about seven hundred dollars in the bank. Would a hundred dollars be all right as a retainer?"

"Make it five dollars," Mason said, grinning, "and give me a check for it. Then you'll be my client. We can talk about fees after we know what we have to talk about. . . . Now, leave me that tissue. Here, put it in this envelope, seal the envelope, write your name on the outside of the envelope so we can keep it identified."

Della Street handed Gwynn Elston an envelope. Gwynn put the tissue in it, sealed the envelope, wrote her name on the outside.

"And again across the flap," Mason said.

Again Gwynn Elson wrote her name across the sealed flap, then looked up and said, "Goodness, Mr. Mason, you're making this just like evidence in a criminal case."

"It may be," Mason said.

She shook her head. "I wouldn't prosecute him, even if he did try to murder me. I just want . . . well, I want to find out what I'm up against."

"You're rather a courageous young woman," Mason said.

She opened her checkbook, made out a check for five dollars, handed it to Della Street, then got to her feet, carefully smoothed her skirt over the hips and smiled at the lawyer.

"You have to be courageous in this business," she told him. "I'll keep you posted, Mr. Mason."

Della Street let her out of the exit door of the office and turned to the lawyer.

Mason said, "Let's phone Paul Drake and alert him, Della, and we'll get John Downey, the toxicologist, to take a look at that tissue just on the off-chance that the bitter taste

16

may not have been all her imagination. Paul can send an operative down to Downey's laboratory."

"Do you think Grimes would have done anything as crude as that?" Della Street asked.

"You can't tell," Mason said. "We're dealing with a man who represents an unknown quantity. We're going to have to find out a lot about that unknown quantity. And we're going to have to find it out fast."

"Do you want to have Paul Drake start some investigative work on Frankline Gillett?"

Mason shook his head. "That would be tipping our client's hand, Della. Paul would be pretty apt to leave a back trail. We're just going to keep hands off until after tonight. . . . Somehow I have an idea that Gwynn Elston can take care of herself. I have an idea she's— Well, she knows her way around."

"And," Della Street said, smiling, "you don't blame Felting Grimes for making passes."

"I'm like Nell." Mason grinned. "I'm broad-minded."

"I noticed the way you looked at her as she walked out," Della Street commented.

"*You* would," Mason told her. "Now, get Paul Drake and see if we can get Downey to give us a quick report on a specific test for strychnine, and be sure he doesn't use up all of the sample in making the test. We're going to have to keep some for evidence."

## Chapter 3

At four-thirty Della Street answered the telephone, said, "Just a moment," arched her eyebrows in Mason's direction and said, "Doctor Downey on the phone."

Mason nodded, picked up his telephone, said, "Hello, John. This is Perry Mason. What did you find?"

"I received an envelope from Paul Drake," Dr. Downey said, "that had the name Gwynn Elston written on the back and again across the flap. I opened that envelope. There was a crumpled piece of tissue on the inside. I cut off about a third of that tissue and subjected it to a test for strychnine."

"What did you find?" Mason asked.

"Strychnine."

"How much?"

"A little more than a trace. Hardly enough to measure, but definitely there was strychnine on the tissue."

"All right," Mason said, "preserve that tissue carefully. Preserve it in the original envelope. Put it in another sealed envelope, lock it in your safe, and be prepared to testify if you have to."

"What's it all about?" Downey asked.

"I don't know yet," Mason told him.

Downey said, "I was afraid I was bringing you bad news because you're usually for the defense."

"No, this is a little different," Mason said. "I'm trying to protect someone."

"Well, if it's this Gwynn Elston," Dr. Downey said, "you'd better put a fence around her, because somebody sure put some strychnine where she got hold of it."

"Thanks a lot," Mason told him. "Just keep that evidence where it can't be contaminated and where you can identify it if you have to."

Mason hung up the telephone, said, "Well, Della, I guess that does it. We'll have to be on call tonight. Give Paul Drake a ring and ask him to come down."

A few moments later Drake's code knock sounded on the door of Mason's private office. Della street let him in.

Drake appraised Della Street with appreciative eyes, said, "Hi, Gorgeous," moved over to the client's big chair, sprawled into his favorite position and grinned at Perry Mason. "Shoot."

Mason said, "I'm expecting an emergency call tonight, Paul."

"Any idea about what time?"

"Sometime between eight-thirty and nine-thirty. A young woman by the name of Gwynn Elston."

"That was the name on the envelope my operative took down to Doctor Downey's office," Drake said.

Mason nodded. "For your information, Paul, that envelope contained a tissue which had very definite traces of strychnine."

"Oh-oh," Drake said, and then after a moment, "What sort of a looker, Perry?"

Della Street held out her hands shoulder high, palms facing each other, and then proceeded to bring the hands down in a series of undulatng curves.

"Like that, eh?" Drake asked.

"Only more so," Della said.

"Darn it, *you* always get the class," Drake complained. "Some woman calls *me* up and wants me to do a shadowing job, or investigate something, and she's always some flat-chested biddy with delusions, hallucinations and frustrations or a sack of cement gone sour. The gals that you represent have upholstery, are easy on the eyes and—"

"And you always get in on the act in the long run,"

Mason said, "so quit crabbing. Now, here's what I want you to do. I want you to be in your office from eight o'clock on. I want you to have your car filled with gas. I want you to have at least one man who is capable of handling anything that may come up; a good, broad-shouldered, husky, two-fisted operative with experience, who can take charge of a situation in case we have to get rough."

"We may have to get rough?" Drake asked.

"I don't know," Mason said.

"Where will you be?" Drake asked.

"At exactly eight-thirty, Della Street and I will be having dinner at the Hollywood Brown Derby," Mason said. "You can catch us there."

"Always the way," Drake said, grinning at Della Street. "I have to be in the office where I can answer the phone. In case I'm hungry, I can have hamburgers and coffee sent up. You and Perry will be sitting out at the Brown Derby toying with one of the specialties of the house."

"The reason for this strategy," Mason said, "is that it puts Della and me a few miles nearer the scene of the projected activity. We may have to get out of there fast and get to the scene of the action. In the event we do, we want to know that you're following up with reinforcements. It's quit raining, but the ground has had a good drenching and the streets are wet. There are more showers predicted. I don't like to drive fast on wet roads."

"All of this sounds mysterious," Drake said.

"It is," Mason said.

"You going to tell me any more?"

Mason shook his head. "I can't. Not right now, Paul."

"Okay," Drake said, resignedly, "I'll play it blind. But I have to meet this Gwynn Elston girl, Perry."

"You will," Mason promised him.

Drake effortlessly uncoiled himself from the chair, got to his feet, winked at Della Street, and left the office.

"You don't think anything will happen before eight-thirty?" Della Street asked.

Mason shook his head. "That's when her appointment with Mrs. Gillett is, and Felting Grimes left this morning and won't be home."

Della Street said, "You have to hand it to that girl for having plenty of nerve, Perry."

Mason nodded.

"And, somehow," Della Street said, "I have an idea that if the going got tough, that girl could be rather dangerous herself."

"What do you mean?" Mason asked.

"Well, she wasn't born yesterday."

"How old is she?" Mason asked.

"Twenty-four or twenty-five, but she's heard lots of questions and knows the answers."

"They all do, these days," Mason said.

"But that girl has plenty of looks and there's something about her, a sort of— Well, you heard what she said, they *all* made passes."

"I thought they all did anyway," Mason said.

She laughed. "You're judging everybody by Paul Drake. . . . I take it we work until eight-thirty."

"Until eight," Mason said. "Then we leave in plenty of time so we can be at the Brown Derby awaiting a call."

"Well," Della Street told him, "if you're going to work after we close up the office, we'd better get to work on that Nelson brief."

Mason nodded, looked at his watch, said, "Let's close up the office now, have a half-hour coffee break, then go to work on the brief."

Mason and Della Street worked until seven-forty-five. Then the lawyer pushed the voluminous file back into the folder and slid it across the desk.

Della Street wearily closed her shorthand notebook,

glanced at her watch, said, "Ten minutes for nose powdering and getting out raincoats."

Promptly at five minutes to eight they closed up the office, walked down to the elevator, and as they came to Paul Drake's office, looked in at the lighted door. Mason said to Drake's switchboard operator, "Tell Paul we're on our way to the Brown Derby. We'll be there from eight-thirty on."

The operator nodded. "Want to talk with Mr. Drake?"

"No, that won't be necessary," Mason said, grinning. "It will just make him envious. Tell him to keep on the job."

Entering the Brown Derby at exactly eight-twenty-five, Mason said to the headwaiter, "Gus, I'm expecting some very important telephone calls. Can you arrange to rush them through to me?"

"I'll do better than that, Mr. Mason. I'll have a phone put right at your table and keep it there, and the switchboard operator will give you a buzz the minute the call comes in."

"That'll be fine, Gus. Thanks," Mason said.

He and Della Street sat at one of the enclosed tables near the wall. Mason had his back turned to the dining room. Della Street was where she could watch the people coming and going. They had one cocktail each, and then a leisurely dinner.

It was nine-fifteen when Mason picked up the telephone and called Paul Drake. "Heard anything, Paul?" he asked, when he had the detective on the line.

"Not a thing," Drake said. "I'm sitting this one out."

"Well," Mason told him, "we'll be dawdling over liqueurs out here for another twenty minutes. Then we'll check with you again."

It was nine-forty when the waiter signaled Perry Mason to pick up his phone.

The lawyer picked up the receiver, and the switchboard operator said, "Mr. Mason?"

"Yes."

"I have a call for you."

A moment later Drake's voice was on the line. "Just heard from your girl friend, Perry."

Mason stiffened. "Any trouble?"

"She was blithe as a lark," Drake said. "Wanted to chat with me for a little while. Wanted to know where you were, and I told her that you were waiting there and she could call the Derby and get connected with you direct. Then she hung on for a few minutes talking about this and that—boy, does that girl have a seductive voice!"

"Hope you didn't try to date her for later on in the evening," Mason said.

"I'm not *that* crude," Drake told him. "This is a business proposition. But I think I disappointed her. She has the sort of voice that indicates she is accustomed to having people make passes over the telephone."

"All right, Mason said, "hang up now. She's probably trying to call me."

"You call me back and let me know if I have to wait."

"Okay," Mason said, "but probably it's all right."

Mason dropped the phone back into its cradle and within less than a minute received another signal from the waiter.

The lawyer picked up the phone, said, "Yes?" and heard Gwynn Elston's voice. "Is this Mr. Perry Mason, the lawyer?"

"That's right."

"This is Gwynn, Mr. Mason."

"Oh, yes, where are you?"

"I'm out at a crossroads service station between Burbank and Chatsworth. There's a little settlement here, Vista del Mesa. I can give you the number if you want."

"Never mind right now," Mason said. "What I want to know is how you came out."

"Everything's fine," she said triumphantly. "I carried it off perfectly. No one suspects a thing."

"Her husband wasn't there?"

"No, of course not, but she said he'd been delayed and

couldn't be there, although she would have liked to have had me talk with him; but they had decided they couldn't afford it right at this time. They had some other expenses and didn't want to incur any more. I told her I was terribly sorry and left, and I didn't try to do any more prying and she wasn't the least bit suspicious. I'm satisfied I carried it off all right. I was there nearly an hour going through the motions of selling her on the idea in case they decided they could afford it later on. That's standard procedure. She was *very* nice to me."

"She wasn't suspicious?"

"Not a bit. You know how it is when you're telling a good, whopping big lie. Somehow you know when it's being taken hook, line and sinker, and then when it isn't, you have that uneasy feeling that there's a little doubt. Then is when the amateur tries to talk fast and cover up the weak points and then gets into trouble by talking too much."

Mason said, "You sound like an accomplished liar."

She laughed throatily. "I am. You'd be surprised how many times a girl has to lie in this world, Mr. Mason."

"All right," Mason told her, "you're satisfied everything's all right now. You're going back to your room?"

"That's right."

"I have news for you," Mason said. "That sample of tissue that you left gave a positive reaction."

She hesitated for several long seconds, then said slowly, "I was almost certain it would. Did you find out about the Chinese characters?"

"Not yet. Does that strychnine alter your plans?" Mason asked.

"It frightens me," she said. "I know now what a heel Felting Grimes is. Someone ought to kill *him*. It would be a good riddance."

"Don't talk that way," Mason said.

"I can't help it. I mean it. . . . And look here, Mr. Perry Mason, I have a bone to pick with *you*."

24

"What is it?" Mason asked.

"I thought you were going to leave things entirely up to me."

"Well?" Mason asked.

"Weren't you responsible for the officer who was waiting out by the gates of the Baxter estate?"

"I was not," Mason said. "Tell me about him."

"Oh, come off it!" she said. "You don't need to pretend with me. This man was from the Drake Detective Agency and he was out there to protect me."

"Tell me about him," Mason said, glancing at Della Street, and holding the receiver partially away from his ear so that Della, leaning forward and putting her cheek close to Mason's, could hear what was being said.

"Well," Gwynn said, "he's very good-looking and very, very nice. I could really go for him. He tried to pretend he needed help but he didn't fool me any. I knew he was out there to protect me. He pretended he'd been standing out in the rain, but his clothes weren't wet at all."

"Where was he, at the Gillett residence?"

"No. He was right by the gates of the Baxter estate. His car had a flat tire and the spare was flat. He wanted to get to a service station so he could have someone go out and fix the tire for him. He was really very nice about it."

"You stopped and talked with him?"

"He flagged me down. He used a spotlight and then showed me his badge and told me he was an officer and said he was in trouble and he wanted to ride with me as far as this little town of Vista del Mesa. That's where I'm phoning from now, you know."

"You gave him a ride?" Mason asked.

"That's right. He stopped off at this service station where I'm phoning. He's making arrangements with the attendant to go on out and pick up his car."

"And what are you going to do?" Mason asked.

"Unless I decide to let this good-looking detective talk

me into a date, I'm going on home. I'm going to tell Nell that I have a headache and go to bed. If you can give me some time tomorrow morning, I'd like to come in and go over this whole business with you."

"All right," Mason said, "I'll see you tomorrow. You're all right now?"

"Oh, absolutely all right."

Mason said, "Now, let me tell you one thing, Gwynn. *Don't* go out tonight with anyone. When you get home, talk with Nell, then go to bed. If Felting Grimes should be there when you arrive, or if he should show up later, *get out of that house at once*. Jump in your car, go to a motel somewhere and call the Drake Detective Agency just as soon as you get located. Do you have that straight?"

"Oh, yes, Mr. Mason. I had made up my mind I'd do something like that in case it became necessary, but Felt won't be home."

"How do you know he won't?"

"Oh, I'm certain he won't. He left on one of his business trips."

"And just how long do those trips take?"

"Usually about a week, but you never can tell. He comes home unexpectedly sometimes."

"This," Mason told her, "may be one of the nights he comes home unexpectedly. You come in to my office in the morning."

"What time?"

Mason glanced at Della Street.

Della, frowningly trying to recall Mason's appointments for the next morning, etched the number ten-thirty on the tablecloth with her forefinger.

"Would ten-thirty be all right for you?" Mason asked.

"Ten thirty? I'll be there, Mr. Mason."

"That's fine," Mason told her. "I'll be expecting you and we'll discuss the case at that time."

The lawyer waited until she had hung up and he had a clear line. Then he called Paul Drake's office.

"Paul," Mason said, when he had the detective on the line, "you didn't have one of your men out there trying to keep an eye on that client of mine, did you?"

"Out where?"

"Out by the George Belding Baxter estate at Vista del Mesa."

"Hell, no, I never heard of it. I followed instructions. I have a man sitting right here in the office all ready to go, all loaded for bear. That's all I've done. Why?"

"I guess it's just a coincidence," Mason said. "Okay, Paul. Call it off for the night but leave word with your switchboard operator that if Gwynn Elston should call, I'm to be notified immediately. I think everything's all right but let's just make sure."

"Okay by me," Drake said, "and I'm to let this operative go now?"

"That's right. Tell him to go home," Mason said. "We're not going to need any strong-arm stuff."

The lawyer hung up the phone, turned to Della Street. "Well," he said, "we may as well call it a day. I guess our pigeon is safe for the night."

Della Street nodded, then said, "Somehow I have an idea your pigeon could put up quite a battle if she had to."

"Probably," Mason said, "but I guess she won't have to. Let's go."

# Chapter 4

At ten-thirty-five Della Street said, "Your bookselling client with the vivid personality seems to be five minutes late."

Mason frowned. "She should be here—but I guess she isn't nearly concerned now that the heat has been turned off."

"Well," Della Street said, "we might utilize the time by dictating replies to those two letters that came in this morning."

"Good idea," Mason said.

The lawyer had finished with replies to the letters by ten-forty-five. He looked at his watch, then at Della Street, frowned and said, "What's the name of that place where she's staying, Della?"

"Felting Grimes, 367 Mandala Drive."

"And they have a phone?"

"Yes, I have the number here."

"Give them a ring," Mason said. "Let's see what the story is this time."

Della Street put through the call, then after a moment, said, "May I speak with Gwynn Elston, please? I believe she's staying there, isn't she? . . . Oh . . . thank you. . . . May I ask who this is talking? . . . Well, thank you very much, Mrs. Grimes. . . . No, never mind. It's just a friend of hers calling on a purely social matter. I won't leave any message. I'll try again later on. Thank you."

Della Street hung up the telephone before Mrs. Grimes could say anything else, and said, "That was Nell Grimes I was talking with. She wanted to take any message; seemed to be rather curious and a little insistent. For your information, Gwynn Elston left at a little before nine this morning and Mrs. Grimes doesn't know exactly what her schedule was or where she can be reached, but she thinks perhaps Miss Elston will call in later on in the morning and if I care to leave a number, she will have her call."

Mason frowned thoughtfully. "Hang it, Della! If anything's happened to that girl, I'm going to be kicking myself all over the office. After all, you know, putting strychnine in a drink . . ."

"But she was there until nine o'clock this morning," Della said, "or shortly before nine o'clock."

"That's what Mrs. Grimes says." Mason said. "I—"

The interoffice phone on Della Street's desk rang sharply. Della Street picked up the instrument, said, "Yes, Gertie. Oh, she is? Just a moment."

She turned to Perry Mason and said, "Your missing client is in the office, safe and sound. And," Della Street went on, looking at her watch, "she's exactly twenty minutes late."

"Tell her to come in," Mason said. "In fact, you might go out and get her, Della, and explain to her that I have to apportion my time rather carefully and when I make an appointment it's—"

"I'll give her a verbal spanking," Della Street said. "Her legs won't impress *me!*" And she vanished.

It was three minutes later when Della Street was back with Gwynn Elston in tow.

Mason looked up and caught sight of Della Street's face, saw the frantic signal she was giving him by blinking eyes rapidly, and turned to Gwynn Elston.

"Well," Mason said, "we seem to—"

"Miss Elston is in serious trouble," Della Street said.

Mason raised his eyebrows.

"I think you'd better sit down, Miss Elston," Della Street said, "and tell Mr. Mason what you just told me."

Mason, studying Gwynn Elston's white, drawn face, said, "I take it Mr. Grimes came home unexpectedly."

She shook her head, tried to say something, stopped, glanced at Della Street, then said, "He won't ever be home any more. He's dead."

"Who's dead? Grimes?"

She nodded.

"All right," Mason said, "how do you know?"

"I saw the body."

"When?"

"About . . . about three-quarters of an hour ago."

"Wait a minute," Mason said, "I was talking with his wife on the phone not ten minutes ago and she—"

"She doesn't know anything about it," Gwynn Elston said. "No one knows. He was murdered."

"Did you kill him?"

She shook her head:

"You'd better tell me about it," Mason said, "and don't take time out to have hysterics, don't do any sobbing, don't wait for me to prompt you. Start talking. Give me just the bare facts. Where did you see him?"

"Out at the George Belding Baxter estate."

"What were you doing out there?"

"I went out to find out about the officer who had given me the gun last night."

"The gun!" Mason exclaimed.

She nodded.

"Go on," Mason told her grimly.

"Do you want me to tell you about the gun, or start at the beginning and—"

"Start at the beginning and talk fast. You went out to see the Gilletts. Mr. Gillett wasn't home. Mrs. Gillett told you she couldn't afford to take on the books right at the present time, what with other expenses they had. You were there almost an hour. Then what did you do?"

"I left."

"All right," Mason said, "what happened then?"

"Well, you remember it had been raining all day. It had rained hard along about dark and then settled down to a cold drizzle. I was driving slowly and when I got to the gates of the Baxter estate I saw this flashlight winking on and off and shining right in my eyes."

"What did you do?"

"At first I started to stop, then I remembered about things and . . . well, I speeded up."

"And then what?"

"Then this man stepped out into the road, right directly in front of me, with the flashlight shining full in my eyes— right into my windshield. So I stopped."

"What sort of a flashlight? A hand flashlight or—"

"One of those hand flashlights, but it was a powerful one; the kind where a big light is mounted right on a battery and—"

"All right, you stopped," Mason said. "Then what happened?"

"This man had his car there. The back of the trunk was up, and he told me he had a flat tire and didn't have a jack and he needed to get to the nearest service station right away so he could have a car come out and change the tire. He said he wanted to ride in with me. He was good-looking but he wasn't wearing a raincoat and his clothes were dry. It had slowed down to a cold drizzle by then but . . . he hadn't been standing there long, that's certain. I think he'd been sitting in his car, just waiting for me to come along. When he saw my lights coming, he got out of the car and went into his act."

"And what did you do?"

"I kept the car door closed and locked. I had rolled down the window just an inch or two so I could hear what he had to say. You see, I've been propositioned in all sorts of ways and—"

"I dare say you have," Mason interrupted. "Never mind that. You had your window down about an inch and a half. Then what happened?"

"He pulled a leather folder out of his pocket and showed me a badge and told me he was an officer and *ordered* me to open up."

"I refused, and he laughed nervously and said, 'Look, I don't have all night to stand here and argue with you. I'm not going to make passes at you. I'm an officer. I'll give you my gun and if I make even the faintest pass at you, you can stop the car and order me out.'"

"Then what did he do?"

She said, "He poked his gun, with the butt first, through the window and it fell down on the seat."

"What did you do?"

"I took the gun and unlocked the door and told him to get in."

"Then what?"

"Then I drove him to that little settlement, Vista del Mesa. It's, oh . . . a couple of miles from the Baxter estate. There was a service station open there, and he said that he'd speak with the attendant about taking a car out."

"All right," Mason said, "what happened?"

"Well, he stopped there, and the attendant was servicing a car so he walked around back in the direction of the rest room and that's when I telephoned you."

"And then?" Mason asked.

"Then I waited and waited and he didn't show up so finally I went to the man at the service station and asked him if arrangements had been made for him to go out and change the tire on the car, and he wanted to know what car, and I said the car that belonged to the man who had just been talking with him. He said no one had been talking with him. He said that he saw me drive up and saw a man get out of the car and go around the back of the station toward the rest rooms and then he was busy with the car he was working on and decided we didn't want any service so he hadn't paid any more attention."

"All right, what did you do then?"

"I asked the man to look in the men's room."

"Your friend wasn't there?"

She shook her head.

"What did you do?"

"I looked in the women's room. He wasn't there. So I drove on home."

"And the gun?" Mason asked.

"I had the gun on the seat beside me."

"All right," Mason said. "You got home. Now, we don't have much time. Let's get this thing straight. What happened?"

"Well, I saw Nell and told her I had a beastly headache and was going to bed and . . . well, I did just what you told me to."

"And you went to bed?"

"I tried to, but Nell came in and said, 'Look here, Gwynn, I don't know what's getting into you, but you're not acting like yourself and for your information you're a rotten liar. Now, sit down and tell me what's the matter. Are you having an affair with my husband? And, if so, is it one of those disastrous things that is going to mean breaking up our relationship? Or is it just a casual cheating that you can both get out of your systems, and I can overlook?'"

"So then you told her the whole business?" Mason asked.

"No, I didn't," she said. "I told her that I wasn't having an affair. I told her that I was a little concerned because I'd been stopped by an officer who had given me his gun and then had gone away and left me with the gun. But I didn't tell her anything about my suspicions, nothing about where I'd been, nothing about you."

"And then what?"

"Well, she tried to cross-examine me. She told me that officers didn't just toss guns into girls' laps and she said she

33

felt certain that Felt had something on his mind and that it had to do with me. She wanted to know if he'd been making any more passes at me and if I'd been letting him get to first base, and— Well, we talked like that for a while and then she seemed very much relieved. She said, 'All right, I'm going to fix you some milk toast and put you to bed and I'm going to go to bed myself.'"

"What happened?" Mason asked.

"We had milk toast and sat and talked for a while and I went to sleep and— Well, I didn't think I was going to be able to sleep. I thought I'd be awake and be nervous but I never slept any more soundly in my life.

"I got up this morning, and Nell wanted to cross-examine me some more and she said the more she thought about my story of the officer and the gun, the more fishy it sounded and that she thought I was holding out on her."

"So what happened?"

"I got the gun and showed it to her and . . . . well, we swung out the cylinder and looked at it. One shell had been fired."

"One shell?" Mason asked.

She nodded.

"Go ahead," Mason said.

"Well," she said, "I didn't say anything to Nell. I tried to pass it all off as a matter of course, but I decided I'd better find out about that officer and who he was, and the only place I knew where I could get a lead was out there at the Baxter estate. He'd evidently been working on a case out there."

"What did you do?"

"I drove out to the Baxter estate. I felt that I had plenty of time to get out there and make inquiries and then get back in order to keep my ten-thirty appointment with you."

"What happened?"

"The gates were open. I drove in and went to the house. I

rang the bell. No one answered. I drove my car around to the back—"

"Why your car? Why didn't you walk?"

"I was afraid of dogs. I wanted to be in the car in case there was a watchdog."

"All right. Go ahead."

"I drove around to the back and didn't particularly want to park the car right in the driveway so I started to turn around and started backing the car. You remember it was raining yesterday, and the grass by the side of the driveway was wet. I got the back tires a little too far off the driveway, and one of the tires skidded; that is, one of the wheels started spinning when I tried to get out. So I left the car right there and opened the door and got out and started to walk to the house, and then I saw a foot sticking out of the tall grass right near the shrubbery and I took a couple of steps forward and could see a man's leg with the pants and the shoe; and then the other leg sort of doubled up, and then I parted the brush and found myself looking into the dead face of Felting Grimes."

"He was dead?" Mason asked.

"Stone, cold dead."

"You touched him?"

"Yes, I leaned forward and touched his face. It was cold."

"What made you think he'd been murdered?"

"There was a bullet hole in his chest," she said.

"All right," Mason told her, "go on. Let's hear the rest of it. What did you do?"

"I got in a panic. I ran back to my car, got in it and tried to start the car. The wheels spun for a moment, then I got onto the driveway and got out of there."

"And the gun?" Mason asked.

She said, "I lost my head over the gun. I slowed the car just as I was going through the gates of the Baxter estate. There was some tall shrubbery over there by the gate, and I got out of the car and threw the gun just as far as I could over into that shrubbery. Then I got in the car again and started driving to Nell's place so I could tell her and . . . and then I remembered my appointment with you so I— Well, here I am."

Mason glanced at his client, then at Della Street, said, "You know, Gwynn, I'm reminded of what your friend, Nell Grimes, said about you."

"What?"

"That you're a rotten liar."

Her face flushed. She started to get to her feet indignantly, then settled back to sit stiffly on the edge of the chair. "I resent that, Mr. Mason."

Mason said, "This story of yours is—"

"Is the truth," she interrupted. "What I resent is being called a rotten liar. I'm a damn good little liar and if I'd been lying I'd have thought up a story that would have been so much more plausible than this that it wouldn't even be funny.

"I know that it sounds strange that an officer would poke his gun through the window of my car so I'd be protected against his advances, but he knew I wasn't going to let him in unless he did something like that and he *had* to get in. He was desperate. . . . I'm telling you the truth."

"All right," Mason said grimly. "You're my client. I'm going to have to act on the assumption that you are telling me the truth. If you're lying to me, you're lying yourself a one-way ticket to the gas chamber. Do you understand that? The most expensive mistake anyone can make is to lie to a lawyer. It's as bad as a patient trying to lie to a doctor. Now, do you understand that?"

She nodded.

Mason said, "There isn't time for me to cross-examine you. There isn't time to check any of this stuff. I'm going to have to play it by ear and I'm going to have to play it fast. I'm going to have to play it on the assumption that you're telling me the truth. Once I start on that assumption I've got to follow it through all the way. If you're lying to me, everything that I do is going to boomerang. Everything I do that is aimed at protecting you is going to work against you. Do you understand that?"

Again she nodded.

"All right," Mason said. "You have a list of prospects that's phoned in every day?"

"Some days it comes by mail."

"You have some prospects to see now?"

"Why, yes, of course. I have a full day ahead of me."

"Get out and call on them," Mason said.

"But aren't I supposed to— Don't we have to report the finding of a body and—"

"Do exactly as I said," Mason told her. "Get out of the office. Start calling on your clients."

"But what about the body?"

"You're supposed to report finding a body. You've reported to me. I'm your attorney. I'll take care of things for you. Understand now, I don't want you to do anything that can be construed as resorting to flight. I want you to go about your business and—"

"And I'm not to tell Nell?"

"You're not to tell a soul," Mason said. "Because of the peculiar circumstances surrounding the death, because of your discovery of the possibility that Nell Grimes is a bigamous spouse and that Felting Grimes is, in reality, Frankline Gillett, and that Mrs. Gillett is the first wife and therefore the legal wife, you're to put yourself in my hands and follow my instructions. I'm telling you to go out and start selling books. Don't telephone in to Nell, don't get in touch with anyone until the close of the day. Follow your regular routine custom and go home when you've finished your day's work."

"As though nothing had happened?"

"Just as though nothing had happened," Mason said. "If

no one contacts you before that time, I will either be waiting for you at the Grimes house or have someone there waiting for you. Now get started."

Gwynn Elston got to her feet, automatically smoothed her skirt down over her hips, started for the door, turned, smiled over her shoulder at Perry Mason and said, "Honestly, Mr. Mason, I'm telling you the absolute truth. If I were lying, it would be a *lot* more artistic."

"Let's hope so," Mason said, as she glided through the door.

Mason nodded to Della Street. "Get down to Paul Drake's office. Tell him we want to know the name of the officer whose car was parked out by the Baxter estate last night. We want to know it fast. We want to know it before anyone else knows it.

"We also want to know what service-station man at Vista del Mesa went out to the Baxter estate and changed a tire on a car.

"Get Paul Drake started. Tell him to put out all the men that are necessary and then to come down here so I can fill him in on details."

"And what about the body?" she asked. "Are you—"

"I'm going to talk with Lieutenant Tragg at Homicide," Mason said. "Tell Gertie to get him on the line as you go through the outer office. Then get down to Paul Drake's office and get busy."

Della Street nodded. "On my way," she said.

Mason waited until Gertie rang, then picked up his phone.

"Well, hello, Lieutenant. How are *you* this morning? This is Perry Mason."

"Yes, your switchboard operator told me," Lt. Tragg said dryly. "I presume you want information?"

"Not at the moment," Mason said. "I want to give you some information."

"How nice of you," Tragg said. "And may I state this is rather a new gambit, Mr. Mason."

Mason said, "This time I want to report what is evidently a murder."

"Well, well," Tragg said, "you *are* taking a new approach! Usually you let us discover the corpse, only to find that— Well, we won't go into that now. Can you give me the name of the murdered man?"

"I believe," Mason said, "the murdered man is Frankline Gillett. He lives out on Tribly Way, near Vista del Mesa. For your information, that is only a short distance from the big estate of George Belding Baxter, which is surrounded, I believe, with an ornamental wrought-iron fence. The body of Mr. Gillett is lying on the grass near the driveway at the rear of the house. It is partially concealed by a bush."

"And how do you know all this?" Tragg asked.

Mason said, "I have a client who discovered the body."

"Where is that client now?"

"I can't tell you, except to say the client has left my office."

"You can't get away with that," Tragg said. "We want to question this client. Get him—or her—back."

Mason said, "The law requires that as an attorney I report a crime when it is brought to my attention. The law does not require my client to make any statements other than to report the finding of the body, nor do I have to disclose the identity of my client.

"Thank you very much, Lieutenant. That will be all."

Mason hung up the phone before Tragg could make any further comment.

# Chapter 5

Paul Drake, moving with an awkward grace which made his motions seem leisurely yet as perfectly timed as those of a juggler or a professional boxer, eased himself into the client's big leather chair, said, "All right, Perry. I've followed instructions and my men are out working. Now I'd like to know the reason for the big emergency."

Mason said, "Get out your notebook, Paul. George Belding Baxter—he has a big place out on Tribly Way. That's where the car was parked last night. What do you know about Baxter generally? I want it quick."

"A big millionaire sportsman," Drake said. "Has a flock of investments, of various sorts."

"How old?"

"About fifty-five."

"Married or single?"

"Single. There was a divorce scandal four or five years ago. She got quite a settlement, a couple of million dollars."

"Find out what you can about him," Mason said.

"Anything else?" Drake asked.

"Lots else," Mason said. "A man by the name of Frankline Gillett lives out on Tribly Way, has a child— Frankline, Junior, aged seven; also a wife. He was murdered last night or early this morning, and the police have been notified the body is in the George Belding Baxter estate."

"The devil!" Drake said. "Who notified the police?"

"I did."

"You?"

"That's right."

Drake started to get up out of the chair. "Hang it, Perry, you can't do things like that."

"Can't do things like what?"

"Notifying the police of a murder and then calling in a detective."

Mason said, "If I *hadn't* notified the police, then what?"

Drake looked at him with an expression of extreme exasperation. "I'm not going to argue with you, I'm telling you."

"All right, I've been told," Mason said. "Now, here's something for your confidential information. I have reason to believe that there may be a thirty-eight-caliber revolver lying in the brush by the gates— Here, I'll draw you a diagram."

Mason made a hasty sketch. "The gun will be in the area around here somewhere."

"What do *I* do?" Drake asked.

"Get out there," Mason said. "If you can't get in the grounds, hang around outside of the fence and keep an eye on that area. If the police find the gun there, I want to know it."

"And if they don't?"

"If they don't," Mason said, "ask the police if *you* can get in and search the grounds. They won't let you, of course, but it will give them ideas."

"Do you want *me* to find the gun?" Drake asked.

"Hell, no," Mason said. "I don't want *you* to find that gun! I'm showing you the place I *don't* want you even looking for the gun. But I *do* want the police to find a gun there. And when they do, I want to know it."

Drake said, "One of these days you're going to get yourself a one-way ticket to the penitentiary."

"Never mind that," Mason said. "Do what I tell you to. I want you to get all the information you can on Baxter. I

41

want you to get all the information you can on Frankline Gillett. I want you to find out everything you can about the murder. I want you to be out there on the job. The police are going to resent your being there. They're going to resent me. You're going to have to use a lot of wits and quite a bit of diplomacy."

"How will I tell them that I knew about the murder and who shall I say is employing me?"

"Tell them I told you about the murder and that I'm employing you," Mason said. "If and when the police find a gun there, I want to know it—fast.

"Now then, here's the low-down on the car I want you to locate. Last night, sometime between nine and ten, this car was stalled out by the gates of the Baxter place. It belonged to an officer or a private detective. Find out everything you can about that car. Get the make of the tires from imprints left in the soil on the side of the road, if you can. Get any discarded cigarette packages, anything that may be a clue. Then I want you to cover all the service stations in Vista del Mesa. I want you to talk with the men who were on duty there last night. I want you to find the one who remembers a young woman who was stood up by her escort there. I want you to get a description of the escort, if possible. And be darn sure the police aren't tailing you when you go to *that* place.

"Then check every service station and tow-car garage out there in Vista del Mesa. Find who it was that went out and repaired a tire on that automobile, get the license number of the automobile, who owned it and who ordered the repairs. Now, that may be quite a job, but I want you to get your men at work on it and do it fast. Use whatever men you need to cover the territory thoroughly and fast."

"I've got my men checking out at Vista del Mesa. They're on their way. They'll phone in for instructions. The car had a flat tire?"

"That's right," Mason said. "Apparently the spare tire

42

was flat. Someone got a service-station man to go out and repair the tire, either put on a new tire or they may have simply pumped up the spare so the man could get away. I want to find out who that man was, and I don't want anyone to know you're—"

The door from the outer office opened, and Lt. Tragg, his hat tilted slightly to the back of his head, entered the room. He was accompanied by a plain-clothes officer who stood two paces back of Lt. Tragg and remained ostentatiously silent.

"That's right, Lieutenant," Mason said, sarcastically, "always feel free to walk right in without knocking."

"We always do," Tragg said cheerfully. "I've explained that you to you before, Perry, particularly on occasions like this. It increases our efficiency."

"You didn't waste any time getting here," Mason said. "I thought *you'd* be out at the Baxter estate."

"I know you did," Tragg said. "That's why I came here. I see you have your detective here, doubtless giving him instructions."

"That's right," Mason said, "and I think I've given him all of them. Go ahead and get started, Paul."

Tragg smiled at Paul Drake and said, "Keep your nose clean, Paul. You have a license, you know, and you wouldn't want to lose it."

"Do sit down, gentlemen," Mason said.

"I don't think we have time for that," Tragg said. "I want to know who your client is in this Gillett murder."

Mason shook his head. "I don't have to tell you that."

"I guess you know the law about making yourself an accessory," Tragg said.

"Sure, I do," Mason told him. "I also know the law about advising clients. And I know the law about concealing evidence. I know the law about reporting a crime. Actually, Lieutenant, I gave you a break. I reported a murder when I didn't have to."

"Oh, yes, you did," Tragg said. "It would have been a crime if you had covered up a murder, having knowledge one had been committed."

"What do you mean by knowledge?" Mason asked. "I didn't see any corpse."

"You knew there was one there."

"Someone told me there was a corpse there."

"Well, that's good enough."

"No, it isn't," Mason said. "That's hearsay evidence. I can tell you right now there's a corpse in the intersection at Seventh and Broadway. You aren't guilty of any crime if you don't rush to the phone, call the police and say, 'There's a corpse at Seventh and Broadway.'"

"That's because there isn't any corpse at Seventh and Broadway," Tragg said.

"How do you know?" Mason asked.

"Because of the tone of your voice, because of a lot of things."

"So you don't have to report to the police?"

"That's right."

Mason said, "Then it becomes a question of how accurately a person can judge the tone of another person's voice. I wish I'd thought of that a little earlier, Lieutenant, because now that you mention it, I'm beginning to think the tone of my client's voice was such that——"

"I know, I know," interrupted Tragg. "Actually I'm only paying you a neighborly call, Perry, because I'd like to have you around. I'd hate to have you shut up where you wouldn't be able to keep in circulation. It would bother you, and I'd miss you."

"And I'd miss you, too," Mason told him. "I always like to have police officer friends who can drop in and tell me what the law is."

"And," Tragg said, "the minute you start aiding and abetting a murderer . . . ."

Mason smiled. "Then I become an accessory. But look

44

through the Penal Code, Lieutenant, and tell me if you find any statute that says it's illegal to aid and abet an innocent person who is wrongfully accused of murder."

*"I'm* talking about a guilty person," Tragg said.

"And *I'm* talking about an innocent one."

"Well," Tragg said, "I'll be moving along, Mason. I dropped in to pay my respects."

"And see if you could catch my client leaving the building," Mason said.

"That, too," Tragg said. "We sewed up the place as soon as we could, but what with traffic conditions and all, I guess your client probably slipped through our fingers. After all, it's a little hard to ask officers to watch the people leaving a busy office building and spot anyone who looks like a client of Perry Mason's."

"Is that what you did?" Mason asked.

"Oh, we did better than that," Tragg said. "We aren't quite that dumb, you know, Mason. We threw out our nets."

"Catch any fish?" Mason asked.

"Got too many," Tragg admitted, grinning. "The boys are screening them now. They have probably a dozen irate customers who are cussing the police up one side and down the other. When you try to do a good job of enforcing the law, the citizens get mad. When you don't enforce it, they write letters to the newspapers demanding a cleanup."

Mason was thoughtful. "I'm afraid I underestimated you, Lieutenant. I thought you'd be dashing out to the Baxter estate."

"Oh, we're doing that, too," Lt. Tragg said. "We cover lots of territory, you know. That particular strip out there along Tribly Way is within the city limits and, therefore, within our jurisdiction, and we have to be reasonably efficient. I'd have been here a little sooner only I personally had to supervise quite a few telephone calls. The elevator operators may be able to give us a little help. We're covering things, Perry. We're getting around."

45

"I'm sure you are," Mason said thoughtfully.

"I'd like to ask you one thing," Tragg went on. "How did your client know that there had been a murder out at the Baxter estate?"

"I'm not certain my client did," Mason said. "Somebody might have told my client there was a body there, and my client might have told me, and I might have advised my client that the best thing to do was to notify the police."

"That, of course, is possible," Tragg said. "Somehow I hardly think it's probable."

"If my client had murdered the man," Mason said, "then I would not have notified the police. I'd have simply advised my client that there was no need to make any statement which might be incriminating, and I would have considered my client's statement one that had been made to me in professional confidence."

Tragg, frowning thoughtfully, said, "Under the circumstances, Perry, the only thing that I can think of is that there's some piece of evidence out there that you're afraid to go after yourself; but you're exceedingly anxious to have the police get hold of it before anything happens to it.

"Now, what kind of piece of evidence would that be?"

"I'm sure I wouldn't know," Mason said.

Tragg turned to the plain-clothes officer with him and said thoughtfully, "It could be the murder weapon, you know, Jim. . . . Well, I guess we've done all the good we can do here. Let's start rolling and see what we can find out, out toward Vista del Mesa. Nice to have seen you, Mason."

"Thanks a lot for dropping in," Mason told him.

"No trouble at all. I always like to drop in when I'm in the neighborhood."

Tragg and the officer left the office.

# Chapter 6

Mason said to Della Street, "Well, Tragg's had time to get out of the neighborhood. He may have delegated someone to keep me under surveillance. However, I want very much to talk with Mrs. Felting Grimes. So you'd better get the car and—"

Mason broke off as the telephone rang frantically, a series of quick, short rings indicating that the girl at the switchboard was trying to give him some signal.

Before Mason could more than motion to Della Street to pick up the telephone, the door opened, and Lt. Tragg and the plain-clothes officer re-entered the office. This time they had Gwynn Elston between them.

"Thought I might surprise you by coming back so soon," Lt. Tragg said cheerfully. "Now, this young woman is Miss Gwynn Elston, Perry. I'm wondering if you can identify her."

Mason, his face a wooden, expressionless mask, said, "Why? Does she want to cash a check?"

"According to the stub in her checkbook," Tragg said, "she's already given a check—a check to Perry Mason for five dollars. That was yesterday."

"You had not right to look in her checkbook or her purse without a warrant," Mason said.

"I know," Tragg said. "I guess occasionally we *do* make our little mistakes; but, you see, it was rather important that we find out about this and— Of course, we don't intend to use it as evidence, Perry."

"That's just the point," Mason said. *"You* think *you* have caught *me* in some technical violation because I don't report a crime even on the strength of hearsay evidence, and then you go and violate all the laws in the books regarding search and seizure and think nothing of it."

"Well, *we're* working in the interests of the justice," Tragg said.

"And how do you know I'm not?" Mason asked.

"Well, that's a question I'm willing to discuss with you," Tragg said. "Now, this young lady seems to be singularly reticent as to just why she gave you a check for five dollars and where she's been during the last hour, and all of that."

Mason said, "Won't you folks sit down?"

Tragg turned to Gwynn Elston and said, not unkindly. "You'd better be seated, ma'am. We'll stand up."

Mason said, "What brings about this visit, Lieutenant?"

Tragg said, "You know, that's the trouble with you brilliant people. You are something akin to a genius, Perry, and you think only in terms of flash and brilliance; you discount good old honest, plodding endeavor.

"Now, take this young woman, for instance. As soon as you telephoned that you were reporting a crime, we just took a few routine precautions. We telephoned the taxicab company that has a stand in front of the building and had them broadcast over the radio that any cab which had picked up a fare in front of this building in the last fifteen minutes was to report by telephone. Then we telephoned the two parking lots that are in the neighborhood and said that any person who had parked a car and left it there within less than an hour was to be stalled when he presented his parking ticket, particularly if he seemed to be in a hurry.

"Well, of course, that's a bad way to do things as far as public relations are concerned. We had to check on two taxicabs that had picked up fares from here. And one poor devil, I guess, missed his plane. He's threatening to sue the city, the police force, the chief and the taxicab company—but we had to check him. We tried to make it as painless as possible—the trouble was, he hadn't allowed himself sufficient time to get to the airport.

"Then there were a dozen people held up at the two parking lots and they were all squawking their heads off. We got down there and sifted them through pretty rapidly until we came to this young woman.

"This young woman didn't tell a very convincing story. She's not a very good liar. I think she's a nice girl and hasn't had much practice. So, after we looked at her driving license and looked her car over and started asking her questions, she suddenly said that she wouldn't answer any more questions until she had seen her attorney. So then, since she had her purse open, showing us her driving license, we took a look at the checkbook and found a stub dated yesterday, showing that a five-dollar payment had been made to Perry Mason.

"Well, now, putting two and two together, we just decided that perhaps this young woman had told you about the body of Frankline Gillet being out at George Belding Baxter's place, and so naturally we'd like to know how she knew about the body."

"And so you asked her?" Mason inquired.

"We did, and she said she'd have to talk with you."

"You felt a five-dollar payment would represent my retainer in a murder case?" Mason asked.

"Not at all," Tragg said, grinning. "That check was yesterday. She consulted you about some little troubles and by today that little trouble had ripened into a murder."

Mason glanced at Gwynn Elston. Her eyes were eloquent and pleading.

Mason almost imperceptibly shook his head.

"Well," Tragg said, "what's the answer?"

"Miss Elston," Mason said, "is a client of mine. I wish to talk to her in private."

"I'm afraid we can't arrange that right now," Lt. Tragg said. "She hasn't been charged with anything yet, but we're questioning her, and I'm quite sure the district attorney is going to want to question her. I think Hamilton Burger, our district attorney, would take a very dim view of the situation if I permitted you to have a private conversation with her right now."

"She's in custody, then?"

"She's in custody to that extent," Tragg said. "Now look, Perry, we don't want to work any injustice in this case. Here is a young, attractive woman who is refusing to answer questions. Now, that's a suspicious sign right on the face of it."

"This," Mason said, "is what comes of trying to co-operate with the police. If I had waited half an hour and then called you—"

"Then you'd have been suppressing evidence," Tragg interrupted. "Oh, you're a smart one, all right, Perry. You know your way around. You could advise your client to do anything that would protect *her* constitutional rights, but as far as you were concerned, as an attorney, having been advised that a murder had been committed, it was your duty to pass the information on to the police immediately. You wanted to keep your skirts clean, so you put through a call to us and got Miss Elston out of your office all at the same time.

"It's just like I say, though, Perry. You brilliant people sometimes underestimate the effect of police routine, of just good old-fashioned legwork and methodical thinking as distinguished from brilliant thinking."

Mason turned to Gwynn Elston. "Miss Elston," he said, "speaking as your attorney, I advise you not to answer any questions of that sort, not to make any statement of any sort until I have had an opportunity to look into the situation. . . . Now, I want to tell you that I *am* looking into the situation. I expect to find out as much as I can about it within the next few hours.

"Lieutenant Tragg will adopt a very fatherly attitude with

you. The officers will tell you that they certainly don't want to work an injustice and if you are innocent they certainly don't want to subject you to a lot of newspaper notoriety. They'll tell you that if you can account for your actions during the past twenty-four hours, they'll be only too glad to turn you loose. They'll tell you all sorts of things to try and get you to talk.

"Just don't talk. Don't say a word. Sit tight. State that I will do your talking for you."

"Well," Tragg said, sighing, "that's all we needed to know, Perry. We just wanted to be sure that this was the client who had told you about the murder. I'm afraid you're going to have to come with us, Miss Elston."

Gwynn said, "Mr. Mason, may I—"

"You may not," Lt. Tragg interrupted. "You're being held on suspicion of first-degree murder."

"And," Mason said, "you are entitled to the benefit of counsel at all times, Miss Elston."

"After she's booked," Tragg said. "Right now we're going to take her to Headquarters for a little interrogation."

"Remember," Mason said to Gwynn, "don't give any answers at all. No matter what questions they may ask, don't answer—not even the simplest questions. Don't tell them where you're living, don't tell them anything."

Mason put a subtle emphasis on the words, "Don't tell them where you're living."

Lt. Tragg held the exit door open and motioned to the officer. "All right, Officer," he said, "we'll take her along. I dislike to do this to an attractive young woman, but if she won't expedite our investigation, she may be held for quite a while."

Mason said, "Don't even give them the time of day, Miss Elston. Your constitutional rights have been violated. They have searched your purse without probable cause."

Tragg grinned back over his shoulder at Mason and said,

"We've got probable cause now, Perry," and stepped out into the corridor.

Mason waited until they were well away from the door, then said to Della Street, "Go down and get my car, Della. Start the motor, stay in the parking lot until ten minutes have elapsed. At exactly ten minutes from now, drive around to the entrance of the building."

"If I can't find a place to stop . . ."

"You won't need to," Mason said. "I'll be waiting at the curb. You do the driving and I'll jump in."

"The Felting Grimes residence?" Della Street asked.

"Exactly," Mason said. "That's the only place where we're one jump ahead of the police. We're going to have to hold that lead."

"But they'll catch up with us?"

"Oh, sure, they'll catch up with us," Mason said. "The only thing that we can hope for is that we can get another lead that will put us another jump ahead of them while we're out there. . . . All right, Della, look at your watch—drive past the office building entrance in exactly ten minutes."

# Chapter 7

Della Street eased the car to a stop at the curb in front of the Grimes residence at 367 Mandala Drive.

"No notes," Perry Mason said, and held the door open for her.

She squirmed out from under the steering wheel, slid along the seat, giving Mason a tantalizing flash of beautiful legs, then stood on the sidewalk shaking her skirt.

"Okay, Chief, let's go."

They walked up the cement walk.

Della Street said in a low voice, "How much are you going to tell her?"

"I don't know," Mason said. "I'm going to play it by ear. We'll have to see what develops."

Mason pressed the door chimes.

Nell Grimes came to the door.

"Good morning," Mason said. "My name is Mason. I'm an attorney at law. This is Miss Della Street, my secretary. We'd like to come in and talk with you for a few moments, if you have no objection."

"*Perry* Mason!" she exclaimed, her eyes widening.

"That's right," Mason said.

"How wonderful! I've read about you in the papers and your face is familiar from pictures. Please do come in."

She led the way into the living room.

Mason said, "I'm going to have to ask you questions. I'm afraid you're going to have to take me on trust."

"Go right ahead," she said. "Ask me anything you want. I'll be glad to help you in any way I can."

"The questions," Mason said, "involve Gwynn Elston."

Mrs. Grimes gave a start of surprise. "Gwynn! Why, what in the world— What's *she* been doing?"

Mason said, "Miss Elston has been rooming with you, I believe."

"Yes. She has her room and eats her breakfast here. Sometimes we invite her for dinner. But the financial arrangements include room with breakfast."

"She's selling books?"

"Yes."

"Do you know anything about where she was last night?"

"Last night," Nell Grimes said, choosing her words carefully, "she was on a most mysterious mission of some sort."

"Did she tell you anything about being stopped by an officer?"

"She told me a story about an officer who stopped her car and tossed his gun in her lap so she could have it to protect herself in case he . . . took liberties."

"Did you believe that story?"

"Definitely not."

"You are friendly with Miss Elston?"

"I've known her for years. She's my closest friend."

"Has she ever lied to you before?"

"She's fibbed once or twice, yes. And I've fibbed to her, but this . . . well, this time it was different."

"She showed you the gun?"

"Yes."

"Swung the cylinder out where you could see it?"

"Yes."

"Did you notice anything unusual about it?"

"Heavens, Mr. Mason, I don't know enough about guns to know the usual from the unusual. Gwynn knows something about guns, but I don't know a thing about them—except what she told me."

"What did she tell you?"

"She said there was an empty shell in the cylinder. I myself saw one of the shells that had this little indentation in the center, which I believe means the shell has been fired. Now, that's all I know about it, except that story Gwynn told me about someone giving her the gun to protect herself with and then running out on her and leaving her with the gun."

"And you didn't believe that story?"

Nell Grimes shook her head. "I'm sorry, I'm not going to lie to you, Mr. Mason. I didn't believe that story."

"Did it ever occur to you that someone might have committed a crime with that gun, knew that it was hot and wanted to get rid of it?"

She thought for several moments, then said, "No, that didn't occur to me. To be perfectly frank with you, Mr. Mason, I had the idea that Gwynn had found herself in some sort of a jam and she had thought up this story about the officer and was trying it out on me to see if it went across."

"You gave her some indication of your disbelief?"

"I certainly did. She knows me well enough to know I wasn't swallowing that for a minute."

"Then where *did* she get this gun, do you know?"

She shook her head.

"You don't know where the gun is now?"

"Gwynn took it with her."

"Do you know where Gwynn is now?"

"No, I haven't heard from her since she left this morning. There was a call for her . . . some woman with an attractive voice who wouldn't leave her number."

"Is your husband home?"

"No. He's on a trip. Sometimes he's away for two or three weeks at a time. Felt—my husband's name is Felting but we all call him Felt for short—is away a lot. He left on a business trip yesterday. He said he'd be gone for a week."

"He travels a lot?"

"Yes."

"By air?"

"Most of the time, yes. However, he has his car, and I have a car."

"Where's your husband's car now?" Mason asked.

"At the airport parking lot, I presume. He left yesterday morning. Why are you asking me all these questions?"

"I am trying to get all the background I can on Gwynn Elston."

"What does my husband have to do with it?"

"Apparently nothing."

"There's one thing, Mr. Mason. . . . I don't know if I should tell you this."

"What is it?"

"Well . . . she went to the medicine cabinet yesterday morning and got some strychnine tablets. Goodness knows what she wanted them for."

"You keep strychnine in a medicine cabinet?"

"Yes. There are no children. We had some trouble with rats and I poisoned some meat."

"Gwynn knew about that?"

"Yes."

"When did she get the tablets?"

"Yesterday morning. Anyway, that's when I found them in her room."

"Where?"

"On the bureau."

"Did you ask her about them?"

"No. I just put them back where they belonged. I intended to ask her but it slipped my mind. She's been acting a little . . . well . . . not normal. She's been lying to me. I'm about half convinced she and my husband have been having a surreptitious affair. . . . After all, if they have, I suppose you can't blame them. She's attractive and she always was something of an exhibitionist. She loves tight sweaters and short skirts—and she lies around half dressed at times.

"And, of course, Felt notices things like that. All men do."

Mason said, "Look here, Mrs. Grimes, I'm going to put some cards on the table with you. Gwynn is in trouble."

"What sort of trouble?"

Mason said, "I don't know how serious it is as yet. The police are questioning her. I want you to help me."

"But what can I do? I'll tell the truth. I'm not going to lie— Can't you tell me any more than that, Mr. Mason? And why the police?"

Mason said, "I want to get all the information I possibly can about what happened last night, everything there is in the way of background, before the police get here."

"The police are coming *here?*"

"The police are coming here," Mason said. "They're going to interview you. They may be here at any time."

"Just what do you want me to do?"

Mason said, "I want you to get out of here."

"To run away?"

"Not that," Mason said. "I simply want you to get in your car and drive. I'll ride in the car with you and talk with you. My secretary will follow behind in my car."

"Where will we go?"

"Just driving around where we can talk without being interrupted."

She reached a sudden decision. "All right, Mr. Mason. I'd do anything that I can for Gwynn. I'll even lie for her. I won't commit perjury in court, but aside from that I'll do anything I can. If you think this will help her, I'll do it."

Mason got to his feet at once. "Let's go," he said. "A police car may pull up here at any time."

Mrs. Grimes led the way out through the back door to the garage. Mason pulled open the garage door. Nell Grimes got in her automobile, raised her skirt so she had plenty of leg room, stepped on the throttle a couple of times, then turned the starter key, put off the emergency brakes and said, "I'll back right out. Your secretary will follow?"

"She'll be right behind us," Mason said.

"What general direction should we take?"

"Just anywhere," Mason told her, "anywhere where there won't be much traffic and where we can talk?"

Nell Grimes backed the car out of the garage onto the driveway, then down the driveway and turned down Mandala Drive.

Della Street followed about a hundred feet behind.

"What did you want to know about, in particular Mr. Mason?"

Mason said, "I would like to have you tell me as much as you can about your husband's business."

"There," she said, "I can be of virtually no help. All I know is that my husband has various business affairs and he never discusses any of them with me. . . . And I still don't see why that would have anything to do with Gwynn."

"You make joint income tax returns?"

"As a matter of fact, we don't. Felt makes his own income tax return. I don't sign it, I don't see it, I know nothing about it."

Mason frowned. "Isn't that unusual?"

"You know more about that than I do," she said. "You're a lawyer. This is my first marriage."

"Do you know George Belding Baxter?" Mason asked.

"Baxter . . . Baxter," she said. "I've heard the name—George Belding Baxter. It has kind of a ring about it, but I don't think I know him, no."

"Do you know if your husband knows him or has done any business with him?"

"No, I don't."

"Do you know the name of the people Miss Elston was calling on last night?"

"Gillett. They live out on Tribly Way by Vista del Mesa somewhere. Didn't Gwynn tell you?"

"Unfortunately," Mason said, "events happened rather rapidly and—"

"Mr. Mason, I want to know. I don't want to go at things blind this way. I want to know what the trouble is. I'm afraid my husband has been playing around with her, and— Tell me, they haven't been picked up together in a motel, or something like that, have they?"

Mason said, "If you've been thinking things like that, hadn't you thought of asking Gwynn to move?"

"No, I hadn't. I'd felt that Felting was going to see lots of attractive girls around and— That's not the way to handle a husband, Mr. Mason. You can't take *all* temptation out of his way."

"But you don't need to have it under his nose," Mason said.

"Well . . . oh, I don't know. I—Gwynn might play around with him but she wouldn't ever steal him."

"Does your husband look at other women—or do you know?"

"Mr. Mason," she said, "you may be able to trust a man not to betray your love, but a man is essentially an egoist and if some smart girl starts making sheep's eyes at him, he thinks he's a great big masculine hero and . . ." Abruptly she reached forward to turn on the dial of the radio.

"How come?" Mason asked, indicating the radio.

She said, "There's a newscast at this hour of local city news. I always listen to it. It's my favorite program. . . . I'll tell you one thing, Mr. Mason, but I'll brain you if you ever repeat it. I know there is some other woman in Felt's life, but I don't know who it is. Up until recently the thought that it might be Gwynn hadn't entered my mind."

"How do you know," Mason asked, "about this other woman?"

"There are a dozen ways, little things . . . and some of them—I'm not going to discuss it with you, Mr. Mason

. . . not in detail, but I do know there's another woman. There has been for some time."

The radio announcer gave a commercial, then commented briefly on the weather and swung directly into the news. "A short time ago, the body of a man who has tentatively been identified as Frankline Gillett was found in the magnificent country estate of George Belding Baxter, the well-known millionaire. The body was lying face up on a grassy strip near the driveway. He had been shot through the heart with a thirty-eight-caliber bullet, and police estimate the time of death at somewhere between nine o'clock and midnight.

"While the man carried a driving license and identification papers in his pocket showing he was Frankline Gillett, of Tribly Way near Vista del Mesa, with his thumbprint on the driving license, police a short time ago discovered an automobile parked near the swimming pool of the Baxter estate. This automobile was registered in the name of Felting Grimes of Mandala Drive, and in the glove compartment police found a leather folder with a complete set of identification cards and a driving license issued to Felting Grimes. The thumbprint on the Grimes driving license was exactly identical with the thumbprint on the Gillett driving license, and police are now . . ."

The rest of the announcer's voice was lost in the scream of tires as Nell Grimes applied the brakes so suddenly that Mason was almost thrown against the windshield. The car skidded into the curb.

Mason, looking back apprehensively, saw that Della Street had barely managed to avoid hitting the rear of the car.

Nell Grimes looked at Mason with wide, shocked eyes. There seemed to be no strength in her jaw. Her hands fell from the steering wheel.

Then suddenly she said, "So that's it! She killed my husband! Do you hear me, Perry Mason? She killed my

60

husband, and you were trying to trap me into taking her part."

Mrs. Grimes's voice rose to the high pitch of hysteria. "That's what she did! She killed my husband! You get out of here, Perry Mason! Don't you ever dare speak to me again. I know now what happened. I— That little hussy took the gun— She planned it that way. She probably thought she was protecting me. . . . Get out of this car! Get out! Get out!"

Mason said, "Now, just a moment, Mrs. Grimes, let's calm down a bit and get this thing straight."

She whirled on the seat, got her legs out from under the steering wheel and started kicking at his face with her high heels. "Get out! Get out!" she screamed. "Get out of this car! I'll kick you, I'll scratch you. I'll kill you! You were trying to get me to betray my own husband. Get out!"

Mason saw the flashing high heels as her feet kicked up at his face. He blocked a couple of kicks as he hastily opened the car door and jumped out to the curb.

"Mrs. Grimes," he said, "you're hysterical. You're jumping at conclusions. Now, if you'll just calm down for a moment . . ."

She whirled around on the seat, depressed the throttle, jerked the car into motion, leaving Mason standing there.

Della Street drove up beside the lawyer and stopped. "Going my way?" she asked.

Mason stood for a moment looking after the speeding car.

"Nice legs," Della Street said. "Or didn't you notice?"

"They were wicked heels," Mason said.

"I'd say she had defended herself that way quite a few times before," Della Street said. "She certainly whirled around and got into action fast. She sacrificed modesty, but she had two wicked weapons. What did you say to her?"

"It wasn't what I said," Mason told her. "It was what the radio announcer said. Police think they have proof that

Frankline Gillett and Felting Grimes are one and the same person."

"And so?" Della Street asked.

"And so," Mason said, "Mrs. Grimes thought I had been trying to trap her into helping the person who had murdered her husband."

"She jumped to the conclusion that Gwynn was guilty?"

"She had been jumping to conclusions before we ever got there this morning," Mason said.

"You should never have let her get those feet up in your face," Della Street said. "Those were wicked heels. She could have gouged an eye out or ripped your face wide open. . . . I should have had my motion picture camera. It would have made a nice shot . . . So what do we do now?"

Mason settled himself on the seat beside Della and said, "Now we're going to drive out to take a look at the estate of George Belding Baxter."

"Paul Drake will be out there?" Della asked.

"Paul Drake will be there," Mason said, "and I think Lieutenant Tragg will have left orders that Paul Drake isn't to be permitted to get anywhere near the scene of the crime, nor to have any chance to uncover any evidence that will do anyone any good."

# Chapter 8

A dozen automobiles were parked along the road near the gates to the George Belding Baxter estate.

Mason found Paul Drake leaning against the wrought-iron fence, smoking a cigarette.

"Where is everybody?" Mason asked.

"Newsmen go inside on a pass," Drake said. "Many other people walk right in. We don't."

"What stops us?"

Drake indicated the uniformed officer at the gates. "He does."

Mason said, "Let's go."

The lawyer, Della Street and Paul Drake approached the uniformed officer. "I want to go in," Mason said.

"Got a pass, press card, anything?"

"I have my professional card," Mason said. "I'm Perry Mason, an attorney at law. I'm representing Gwynn Elston, who is being questioned concerning the murder here."

The officer said, "Get a pass and I let you in."

"Where do I get a pass?"

"It depends. Some of the passes are signed by Lieutenant Tragg of Homicide, some by the sheriff's office, and you get in with a press card. That is, you don't get into the house but you get into the grounds."

"Nice," Mason said. "Any communication with the house?"

"What do you mean?"

"Lieutenant Tragg's in there now?"

"I'm not supposed to be giving out information about Lieutenant Tragg."

"I'd like to reach him."

"So would lots of other people."

"You don't have any telephone communication?"

"We don't carry portable walkie-talkies around with us, if that's what you mean."

"See what I mean?" Paul Drake asked. "We're the public. We're an excluded class."

"I see," Mason said.

The lawyer took a hammered silver cigarette case from his pocket, opened it, extended it to the officer. "Have one?" he asked.

The officer shook his head.

Mason extended it to Della Street, who said, "No, thanks."

Drake took a cigarette.

Mason produced a lighter, held it for Drake's cigarette, lit one himself, snapped the cigarette case closed and casually tossed it high over the wrought-iron fence into the shrubbery.

"Hey, what's the hell's going on?" the officer said.

Mason said, "What's the matter, Officer"

"You can't throw things in there."

"Some law against it?" Mason asked.

"Sure, there's a law against it. You can't throw refuse around on other people's property."

"Come, come," Mason said, "that's not refuse. That was a very valuable cigarette case. Now take a look at this. This is a very fine cigarette lighter."

The lawyer casually tossed it over into the bushes.

"Well, Paul," he said, "I guess there's not much we can do here."

"Hey, wait a minute," the officer ordered. "What's the idea? What are you trying to do?"

"Nothing," Mason said. "I've already done all I intended to do."

"You can't plant evidence."

"Evidence of what?"

"I don't know," the officer said.

"I'm sure you don't," Mason agreed.

The officer walked over to the police car which was parked near by just inside the gates, tuned in on Headquarters, held the transmitter close to his lips and talked for some time, then listened apparently to instructions.

The officer at length hung up the transmitter, got out of the car and came over to Perry Mason, glowering at him belligerently. "You said your name was Perry Mason, the lawyer?"

"That's right," Mason said.

The lawyer stretched, yawned, took a great drag at the cigarette, gave Drake a surreptitious wink and said, "Well, let's go, Paul."

"You can't go now," the officer said.

"What?" Mason said. "You mean I'm not free to leave here?"

"You stick around a minute."

"Are you going to let me go in?"

"No."

"Then there's nothing further I can do here. I'll be leaving."

"I said you wait. Lieutenant Tragg wants to talk with you."

"When I wanted to talk with him you told me lots of people wanted to talk with him. Now you tell me he wants to talk with me. For your information, lots of people want to talk with me."

"Now, take it easy, buddy," the officer said. "You've been planting evidence out here."

"Evidence of what?"

"Well, you've been throwing things over the fence."

"Now, with that," Mason said, "I agree with you, and I would like the opportunity to go and recover my personal property."

The officer looked anxiously back along the driveway.

A few moments later, Lt. Tragg, accompanied by a plain-clothes detective, came striding down the graveled walk.

"Well, well," he said, "we seem to have quite a collection here: Miss Street, Perry Mason, Paul Drake."

Tragg turned to the officer. "Now, what's the trouble, Officer?"

"This guy," the officer said, pointing at Mason, "takes a cigarette case out of his pocket, offers a cigarette around, then casually tosses the whole case over the fence into the shrubbery. Then, when I tell him he can't do that, he takes a cigarette lighter and throws it over after the cigarette case."

Tragg's eyes narrowed. "Now, you've been watching him all the time he was here?"

"That's right."

"Those two things are the *only* things he threw over there?"

"That's right."

"What about him?" Tragg asked, pointing at Paul Drake.

"He's been hanging around here for an hour."

"What's he been doing?"

"Oh, just loafing around."

"Anywhere near this wrought-iron fence?"

"Standing right up against it, smoking and—"

Tragg said angrily, "Smoking and planting evidence. He's the one that planted stuff in there . . . Now, let's find out what this is all about. What Mason did was simply a grandstand. You shouldn't have let this Paul Drake hang around that fence."

"Well, you said not to let anybody inside. He was out-side."

"Use your head," Tragg said. "Anybody could lean against that fence, put his hand behind his coat, and when you weren't looking, throw something in the brush in there."

"Throw what?" the officer asked.

"How the devil do I know!" Tragg said. "But I'm going to find out. Let's go take a look. Now, where did Mason throw this cigarette case and lighter?"

"Right over in there. I saw the light glint on it a minute ago. If you'll move around here, you can see— Hey, there it is. You can see the reflection of the light on it."

Tragg said to the plain-clothes officer, "All right, Dick, go in there and I'll direct you to it. While you're in there, look around."

Tragg stood thoughtfully watching Mason.

The officer at the gate said, "A little more to the right . . . a little farther back . . . now, just a bit to the right. There you are, you're right over it."

The plain-clothes officer called out, "I have the cigarette lighter, Lieutenant."

"The cigarette case went a little farther and a little more over to the right," the officer called. "I watched it when it hit. It hit on one of the tree limbs and bounced. It's—"

"I see it," the man called. "I've got it and. . . ."

"All right, what else?" Tragg asked as the officer's voice suddenly ceased.

"There's a gun here, Lieutenant."

"I thought so," Lt. Tragg said. "*That's* the reason for all these shenanigans. Paul Drake planted the gun, and Mason wanted to be sure we found it."

"That's making rather a broad accusation of unprofessional conduct against a reputable private detective, Lieutenant," Mason said.

Tragg thought a minute and said, "Okay, okay, I was just thinking out loud. I wasn't talking to anybody in particular. Ignore it, you fellows. Put a pencil down the barrel of that gun, Dick, and bring it out here. Let's have a look at it."

The plain-clothes officer scrambled out from the brushy

hedge and shrubbery holding a .38-caliber revolver by means of a pencil which had been pushed down the barrel.

"Now, what do you know," Lt. Tragg said, taking hold of the pencil and looking at the revolver carefully. "All right, let's get this down to the laboratory and see what we can discover. Maybe we can find something that will tie it in with the person who planted it here."

"And my cigarette case and lighter?" Mason asked. "Do I get them back?"

Tragg grinned at him. "You don't get them back," he said, "not for a while, anyway. And when you get them back, they'll have my initials scratched on them . . . You see, Perry, these have become evidence in the case."

"In the meantime," Mason said, "what do I do for smokes?"

"Just a plain package of cigarettes works very well for us officers," Lt. Tragg said, "and a folding book of paper matches accomplishes the ignition job very nicely. And now, Officer, we're going to get a rope and stretch it across the roadway between these two gates and keep everybody away from that iron fence."

"Locking the stable after the horse has been stolen?" Mason asked.

"Just checking the people who are planting evidence," Lt. Tragg said. "We don't want them to plant so much that we get *too* big a crop."

"That's right," Mason told him. "And, in the meantime you'd better look around in there and see if there isn't another cigarette lighter and another cigarette case."

"And another gun," Tragg said thoughtfully. "You know, Mason, sometimes your thinking parallels mine to a remarkable degree. Dick, get a rope and we'll just rope this whole thing off, and Officer, keep everybody away from that fence. We don't want anyone loitering around here."

"That," Mason said, "is our cue, Della. That's our exit line."

"Sometimes," Tragg said, "you take a hint beautifully, Mason. I wish I knew why you were so anxious to have us find that gun and I also wish I knew how you knew the gun was there."

Mason turned to Drake and said, "That's what comes of being a police officer, Paul. It makes you cynical and skeptical. I toss a cigarette case on the waters and it comes back a gun."

"You bird-dogged some evidence for us, all right," Tragg said, "but we still can't evaluate it and don't know just what it amounts to."

"When you find the second gun," Mason told him, "you might have something."

"I'll tell you one thing," Tragg promised. "We're going to trace this gun from the time it left the manufacturer until the time it was planted here in the grounds, and if that gun is connected with you in any way, you're going to hear about it."

"Illegal to toss a gun on private property?" Mason asked.

"Illegal to falsify evidence," Tragg said.

"Come, come, Lieutenant, you'd better read your Penal Code again. What's false about it and how does it happen to be evidence?"

Tragg jerked a thumb toward the parked automobiles. "On your way," he said, "there's nothing more for you here."

Mason turned to Della Street. "In view of the situation here, Della, let's go buy some cigarettes. Come on, Paul, we'll buy you lunch."

# Chapter 9

It was shortly after four o'clock and Mason and Della Street were back in the lawyer's office when Paul Drake came in with a series of reports.

Mason, who had been impatiently pacing the floor, paused as Paul Drake produced the sheaf of flimsy from the Bristol board file and said, "Okay, Perry, we're trying to keep one jump ahead of the police, but it's a job."

"What do you mean, one jump ahead of the police?" Mason asked. "They've caught up with us by this time."

"No, they haven't," Drake said. "I had a break, Perry."

"Go ahead," Mason said, "what's the break?"

"I wanted to find out whether Gillett and Grimes was the guy's right name," Drake said, "so I did something the police apparently neglected to do. I looked up the birth certificates of Felting Grimes and Frankline Gillett. There isn't any birth certificate for Felting Grimes, but there is a birth certificate for Franklin Gillett. Now, I'm going to skip over all the immaterial matter and just hit the high spots, because some of this is red hot and you may want to take action."

"Go ahead," Mason said.

"Frankline Gillett's father was Gorman Gillett. I guess his father ran off, when he was just a youngster. The mother filed suit for divorce on the ground of desertion, then the mother died. No one seems to know what happened to Gorman Gillett—that is, as far as the divorce records were concerned.

"Now, here's a funny one, Perry. Gorman is an unusual

name. I checked the vital statistics and, of course, I have a bunch of operatives out working on the case.

"One of these chaps has a mountain cabin up at Pine Haven. That's a mountain town up near the Walker Pass country. He says there was a character up there named Gorman Gillett, who was something of a recluse. He—"

"*Was?*" Mason interposed.

"That's right," Drake said. "My operative put through a phone call and finds that the fellow died three days ago. The coroner and public administrator up there can't find any relatives, and he's holding the body, hoping someone will show up and pay for a funeral.

"Now, Gorman is an unusual name and there's just a chance—the age is about right and everything would seem to fit."

Mason frowned in thoughtful contemplation as he digested the news. "How well did your operative know him, Paul?"

"Not too well. The fellow was a character up there. He'd let himself get pretty much run down. That is, he wore old ragged clothes, grew a beard, didn't shave or have a haircut for long periods of time, and no one knew just how he subsisted."

"And no relatives?"

"No relatives."

"What else have you got—anything?"

"A lot of routine stuff. I've got a picture of Frankline Gillett."

"What about Mrs. Grimes?"

"Oh, she got in touch with the police right after she left you, told them a story about how you were trying to get her to go into hiding and . . . what with one thing and another, I guess you're going to get your name in the papers, Perry."

"You have a copy of the driving licenses?"

"That's right. Frankline Gillett was five feet, eleven

inches tall, thirty-two years old, weighed a hundred and eighty-five pounds, had brown hair and hazel eyes. I got a copy of his photograph from the newspaper boys, but it'll be out in the paper within a couple of hours."

"What about the car with the flat tire in front of the gates of the George Belding Baxter estate?" Mason asked.

"There wasn't any," Drake said. "You may as well face that fact now as later."

"How come?" Mason asked.

"There wasn't any such car."

"There had to be," Mason said.

Drake shook his head. "Not with any flat tire, at any rate."

"How do you know?"

"First, we have negative proof," Drake said, "for what it's worth. I've covered all the garages, all the automobile clubs, all of the service stations within the area. No one sent a tow car or a repair car out there. I've had my men check with the service station where you asked me to check, and there's no question that a young woman who answers the general description of your client showed up there last night about nine-thirty. The fellow remembers the time because he went off work at ten o'clock and it was just about a half hour before his relief showed up.

"The woman was driving the car. The man got out and made some inquiry and walked around the back of the service station and apparently disappeared."

"Description of the man?" Mason asked.

"I have it here. About five-eight-and-a-half or five-feet-nine, about twenty-five years of age, weight about a hundred and seventy-five pounds. He had very dark, wavy hair, but the service-station man couldn't give me the color of his eyes. He was dressed in a dark brown suit.

"Now then, notice the time, Perry. It's fixed rather accurately at nine-thirty. At ten o'clock the caretaker at the George Belding Baxter estate closed the iron gates and locked them with a chain. At that time, there was no car parked in front of the gates."

"Who's this caretaker?" Mason asked.

"A character by the name of Corley L. Ketchum. He has a little cottage back in the grounds and it's his duty to see that the gates are opened at seven o'clock every morning and closed at ten o'clock at night."

"Who takes care of the house?" Mason asked. "They certainly don't let anyone just come walking in, do they?"

"No. When George Belding Baxter is there, he has a couple of servants who come in at eight o'clock in the morning and leave at five o'clock in the evening. Then there's a cook who comes at noon and works until eight o'clock and a housekeeper who lives on the premises. The housekeeper is supposed to be there most of the time, but today is her day off and she told police that George Belding Baxter had told her she could leave the night before. She left somewhere around nine."

"What about Baxter?" Mason asked. "Where is he?"

"Baxter had been up in San Francisco on a business deal and he was driving back. He got as far as Bakersfield, checked in at a motel, spent the night, then came on here this morning. He drove directly to his office and the first he knew anything was wrong out at the estate was when police contacted him at the office."

"He's seen photographs of the body?" Mason asked.

"He's seen the body itself," Drake said. "He says the man is a complete stranger to him. He's taking a plane for Honolulu tomorrow. He's left word for his employees to give the police every co-operation, and I understand he's turned over the keys to Lieutenant Tragg.

"The police feel reasonably certain now that Gwynn Elston knew Frankline Gillett and Felting Grimes were one and the same person—at least by the time she had seen a picture of Frankline Gillett on her first trip out to the Gillett residence.

"The police theory is that Grimes caught up with her after her visit with Mrs. Gillett, that she got in his car, that she probably accused him of being a bigamist and there must have been quite a scene. So then she pulled a gun on him, forced him to drive into the George Belding Baxter estate and herded him, at gun point, into the driveway, killed him, and—"

"And how did she get home?" Mason asked.

"Walked to her car," Drake said. "At any rate, that's the theory of the police; that she had parked her car somewhere, that Grimes caught up with her, that she went in his car and forced him to drive into the Baxter estate. That's where the shooting took place. Then your client dumped the body, parked the Grimes car and walked back to where she had left her car. This all had to be done before the gates at the Baxter estate were closed."

"How about the man who was with her at the service station, Paul?"

"Her boy friend; an accomplice. Just as soon as the police find out about him they'll have a dead open-and-shut case."

"It's open," Mason said. "They can't shut it."

"Don't kid yourself," Drake said. "You just watch the way they go about tying up the loose threads."

Mason was thoughtfully silent for a few moments, then said, "It seems a shame that my second cousin, Gorman Gillett, has no one to bury him. I'm sorry to learn of his death, Paul. I guess I can put up the money for his funeral all right."

Drake's face showed alarm. "Now, wait a minute, Perry. Don't get yourself caught in *that* trap."

"Why not?" Mason asked.

"It's illegal. You can't— You don't dare to claim the man was your relative."

"I know of no law against it," Mason said. "I certainly can put up burial fees if I want."

"But you can't tell them he's a close relative and claim the body."

"Who wants the body?" Mason asked. "Let's just go take a look."

"It's time wasted," Drake said. "You're one jump ahead of the police because you know where Gillett's father is, but Frankline had lost track of his father for years and years; in fact, ever since he was a kid."

"How do you know he had?" Mason asked.

"Well, that's the story he told everybody."

"He told lots of stories," Mason said. "He told his wife he was away on business and apparently drove away and just moved into the Felting Grimes home. Then, when he got tired of living there, he'd tell Nell Grimes he was going away on business and go back to the charms of Mrs. Gillett. . . . Poor old Gorman, he's certainly entitled to a decent burial, and I have an idea that if I'm not around where the police can throw questions at me tonight, I may be just as well off."

Drake said, "This is one time I am going to be tickled to death to stay right in my little cubicle, keep on the job, have lukewarm coffee and eat soggy hamburgers that have been sent in to me from the hole-in-the-wall restaurant downstairs."

Mason turned to Della Street. "Want a ride, Della?"

"I'd love it."

"Bring a notebook, a few pencils," Mason said. And then, after a moment, added, "You'd better get a lipstick that's as light in tint as possible—and we'd better get started. They probably roll up the sidewalks in Pine Haven at eight o'clock. . . . What have the police found out about the gun, Paul?"

"Anything they've found out so far they haven't released. But they're sure checking it. I think they have something pretty hot, but they don't want anything to leak out just yet . . . Look, Perry, suppose Gorman Gillett *should* be the father of Frankline Gillett—then what?"

"Then," Mason said, "you have to admit that the mortality in the family suddenly became rather high. If two members of the family perished within a matter of twenty-four or thirty-six hours, you have to admit it's a startling coincidence."

Drake said, "Gosh, Perry, I never thought of it from that angle."

"It may not be an angle," Mason said. "It may be a curve." He turned and nodded to Della. "Come on, Della, let's give the car some exercise."

# Chapter 10

Pine Haven was high enough to retain its pure mountain air while the lowlands were filled with murky atmosphere. Stars blazed steadily down from a crystal-clear sky while lofty pines and firs presented black silhouettes towering up against the stars.

A colored light shed illumination over the entrance of the Bolton Funeral Home. In the front, there was a small chapel on one side, an office on the other and behind them, a huge, rambling building which had once been an ornate residence.

A gasoline station and an ice cream parlor were open. A corner drugstore was just closing. A few stragglers emerged from the motion picture theater. Aside from that, the small mountain town was all tucked in for the night.

Mason parked the car in front of the Bolton Funeral Home, walked up to the office which had gilt lettering on the glass reading: ASSISTANT TO THE CORONER AND PUBLIC ADMINISTRATOR.

Mason pressed the bell button.

Within a very few seconds the door was opened by a whimsical-looking individual in his early sixties, with steel-rimmed glasses, wiry, unruly hair, a drooping, gray mustache, and rounded shoulders.

"I'm looking for Mr. Bolton," Mason said.

"You've found him."

Mason extended his hand. "My name is Mason," he said. "This is Miss Street. I understand you have a body here and no relatives have shown up to claim it."

"Gorman Gillett?" Bolton asked.

"That's right."

"You a relative?"

"I don't know," Mason said. "There is a possibility. I may say, however, to be perfectly fair, that it's a *remote* possibility. However, I came up here to take a look at the corpse. If this is the man I think, and if there are no other relatives, or perhaps I should say if no relatives show up to claim the body, I would at least like to arrange for the funeral expenses."

Bolton looked at Mason over the top of the steel-rimmed glasses. "Well, now, *that's* something!" he said. "Come in."

A smell of incense, flowers and embalming fluid mingled in the close air of the interior.

"Been working on my books," Bolton explained, "and was just about getting ready to turn in—gets a little chilly up here at night and I didn't want to turn on the central heating plant, so it may be just a little nippy. Now, tell me, Mr. Mason, just what did you have in mind?"

"Something rather simple and inexpensive," Mason said, "but not exactly cheap."

"You'd want to move the body?"

"I would prefer not to claim the body," Mason said. "My function in the case would be to make a sufficient financial contribution to see that there was a modest but decent funeral."

"Well, now, that's right nice," Bolton said. "Would you like to look at some of the caskets?"

Mason said, "I'd be inclined to leave that to you. However, all I have to go on at the moment is a name. I wonder if I could look at the body?"

"Sure thing," Bolton said. "Now, you might be sort of shocked, Mr. Mason, and I don't think the young lady would like to look at it—this isn't like one of the occasions where we have a lot of relatives, a nice casket and things all fixed up in the slumber room. As a matter of fact, things are sort of at odds and ends here. Haven't had a funeral for four days and there isn't anyone in the slumber room now. I've— You let me have just a minute or two, will you? Then you can go in."

"Certainly," Mason said.

Bolton jumped up from the desk and scurried through a door.

Mason said, "You stay here, Della. I'll tell him to get a check from you. We'll go up to about three-fifty—Give me that light-colored lipstick."

"Just what did you have in mind?" Della Street asked.

"I don't know," he said. "You'll have to follow my signals."

She said, "You got a five-dollar retainer in a case, you obligate yourself to pay the Drake Detective Agency about twelve hundred and fifty dollars right off the bat, and then you come up here and gamble three-fifty on a funeral for an unknown corpse."

"Sounds exciting, doesn't it?" Mason said.

"Perfectly disastrous from a bookkeeper's standpoint," she told him.

"How does the Internal Revenue Department feel about practicing law at a loss?"

"They take a dim view of it. Expenses are supposed to be ordinary, necessary and, I believe, reasonable."

"Money," Mason said, "was made round so it can be kept in circulation. Did you ever realize, Della, that if I take a dollar and pay it to Paul Drake, and Drake pays it to his landlady, and the landlady pays it to the grocer, that dollar is doing a man-sized job in the economy? Whereas, if I put the dollar in my pocket and sit on it—"

Della Street interrupted. "If you ever put a dollar in your pocket and sat on it, it would burn a hole in your pants pocket. So just keep on spending the way you do. It saves wear and tear on pants and anatomy."

"Thanks," Mason said. "I just wanted you to know I'm contributing to the economy of the country."

"You're supporting it virtually unaided as far as I can determine."

The door opened, and Bolton came back. "Like to take a look, Mr. Mason?" he said. "Right this way."

Bolton led the way back through a passageway, turned into a door marked SLUMBER ROOM.

This room had subdued rose-colored lighting. There was the heavy smell of perfume, and soft music seeped through hidden loud-speakers.

Bolton smiled apologetically at Mason. "Just turned on the recorded music," he said. "Haven't got the volume quite right—the player is cold and it increases its volume a little as it gets warmed up.

"Now, I haven't had a chance to move him into the slumber room. He's out here in the place I keep for county cases. But I guess you won't mind."

"Not at all," Mason said. "I just wanted to look at him."

Bolton led the way to a marble slab, turned down a sheet.

"This is old Gorman Gillett," he said, "something of a philosopher. . . . Of course, I cleaned him up a little—gave him a shave—peculiar sort of a codger, would always talk with you about philosophy and things of that sort—had a little cabin up here and kept it piled up with all sorts of junk—just never seemed to do any work to speak of. On the other hand, I guess he never spent very much money—get himself a sack of flour once in a while and come deer season he'd go out and get a buck so he could make it into jerky—always seemed to have a supply of jerky. One deer would last him all year."

Bolton's right eye closed behind the tilted spectacles in a slow wink.

Mason stood looking down at the corpse, serene in the tranquillity of death.

"That the man you're looking for?" Bolton asked.

Mason slowly nodded. "I can't be certain, of course, but I'm willing to gamble— What sort of a funeral could I get for three hundred and fifty dollars?"

"For three hundred and fifty dollars," Bolton said "we could give you a very, very nice job, Mr. Mason, very nice indeed. That would include a minister, a singer and transportation to the grave for you and Miss Street."

Mason stood studying the corpse. "Would you mind stepping out and asking Miss Street if she has her checkbook?" he said. "And if she does, ask her to make you a check for three hundred and fifty dollars."

"I certainly will," Bolton said. "I'll do it right away."

Bolton's short, quick steps sent him hurrying to the door like a baby quail scuttling for cover.

As soon as the door had closed, Mason took out the lipstick, threw back the sheet, picked up the cold hand of the corpse, rubbed lipstick over the finger tips, then pressed the finger tips to a folded piece of paper which he took from his pocket.

Having done that with the right hand, he proceeded to do it with the left, making certain that he had legible fingerprints, paying particular attention to the thumbs, which he rolled carefully along the paper.

Glancing at the door, he took another sheet of paper from his pocket, made another set of fingerprints, then with a handkerchief wiped the fingers of the corpse and pulled the sheet back up.

Then Mason walked to the door leading to the other room.

Della Street, obviously trying to give Mason all the time that he needed for whatever he planned to do, said, "I'm sorry, I messed up one of the checks and had to tear it up and begin all over again."

"That's fine," Mason said. "Just make a note on the stub."

"I did."

Della Street handed Bolton the check.

Bolton looked at it, started to put it in his pocket, then suddenly did a double take and said, "You're Perry Mason."

"That's right."

"The lawyer?"

"Yes."

"Well, now, Mr. Mason, I didn't know this man was a relative of yours."

"I didn't say he was," Mason said. "I said that he *might* be a relative of mine."

"Well, now that you've seen him," Bolton asked, "what do you think?"

Mason said, "You have a check. I thought enough of him to arrange for a funeral."

Bolton thought things over a moment, then slowly folded the check and put it in his pocket.

"Always like to deal with people who put things on a business basis," he said. "Now, just what was it you wanted, Mr. Mason?"

"Where did Gillett live? You said there was a cabin out here?"

"That's right, about two miles out, a little cabin . . . Like to take a look?"

"I'd like to take a look."

"Got to get my wife to mind the place," Bolton said. "Just a minute, I'll go tell her and then I'll go with you."

"You got a key?" Mason asked.

"Sure. I'm deputy public administrator up here, and so far there aren't any relatives."

"Is there any estate?" Mason asked.

"Not enough to bury him," Bolton said. "Guess you'd like to take a look around, wouldn't you?"

"Well," Mason said, "I am anxious to establish the real identity of the corpse."

"Sure, sure," Bolton said. "You got a three hundred and

fifty dollar investment. You want something in return. I wasn't born yesterday. Mr. Mason and I ain't going to die tomorrow. Now, you just sit right there for a minute and I'll go tell the wife she's got to run the place—not that I'm expecting anything. Fellow by the name of Jones up here was pretty sick, but I think he's pulling through. Old Grandma Harper is pretty low, but she's hanging on. Woman in a nursing home up here, though, may go any minute . . . It'd surprise you how people pick out odd times to go, Mr. Mason. Right around two or three o'clock in the morning you're apt to get quite a few calls— Well, you wouldn't be interested in that. You want to take a look in the cabin. All right, I'll tell the wife and then we'll go."

Once more Bolton scurried through a door and disappeared.

"Get what you wanted?" Della Street asked.

Mason showed her the fingerprints.

"What will they prove?" she asked.

"I haven't the faintest idea."

"Think the police will get up here?"

"The police," Mason said, "are dogged and thorough, painstaking and smart. But there's a darn good chance we are way ahead of them on Gorman Gillett."

"And how do *you* expect to find out what *you* want to know?"

"We're going to exhaust the local sources of information," Mason said.

"Meaning Bolton?"

"Meaning Bolton."

The door opened, and Bolton came in, struggling into an overcoat and dangling a key to which was attached a chain, which, in turn, was fasten to a circle of metal on which was stamped a number.

"Actually haven't taken physical inventory yet," Bolton said, "just looked around. But you folks come along and we'll see if we can find something that'll convince you just who the guy was."

"You may just as well go in my car," Mason said. "It's out here in front and all ready."

"That's fine," Bolton told him. "You just go right down this main street four blocks, then you turn to the right and— We have to go up a little grade and it's inclined to be slippery. We've had a little rain up here and the road gets slick. Miss Street isn't nervous, is she?"

"Miss Street is not nervous," Mason said dryly.

"Well, that's fine. Some women are."

Bolton started to get in the back seat. Mason said, "We can sit three in front. It'll be better that way. I can turn on the heater and have the car warmed up in a jiffy."

Della Street stepped with smooth grace into the car, slid over to the center of the front seat.

Bolton got in beside her, looked at her over the tops of his steel-rimmed glasses with appreciative appraisal.

Mason started the car, drove down the street for four blocks, then said to Bolton, "Turn to the right here?"

"That's right. Turn to the right here, cross the bridge over the creek, then we do a little climbing. Just don't get to fighting the road and it'll go all right. Just keep your wheels moving and take it easy."

"Thanks," Mason said.

The car moved along a dirt road, rumbled across a wooden bridge, then started climbing slowly and steadily.

After a minute or so, Bolton heaved a sigh and relaxed against the seat.

"See you've driven mountain roads before, Mr. Mason. I asked you about Miss Street—as a matter of fact, I'm a little nervous myself when I get out on these roads with a city driver."

"You feeling all right now?" Mason asked.

"Fine," Bolton said. "I see you've done lots of mountain driving."

"How did Gillett happen to die?" Mason asked. "What was the cause of death?"

"Coronary occlusion, according to the doctor's certificate."

"You know the doctor that attended him?"

"Sure, sure," Bolton said. "Old Doc Carver—Ewald P. Carver."

He twisted his head to one side with a quick, birdlike gesture, glanced up at Della Street, then across at Mason and said, "Of course, Mr. Mason, since you're a cash customer, we try to accommodate you. Now, you understand what we mean up here by an attending physician?"

"One who attended the deceased at the time of death?" Mason asked.

"Well, now, we don't necessarily have to go that far," Bolton said. "You see, it's kind of a job having an inquest up here, and the words 'attending physician' can mean lots of things. Now, if you go to see a doctor or a doctor sees you and you've got heart trouble and he treats you for it, and then you turn up dead, there's no need to cut you open and mess around in your insides—and that makes an awful messy job for a mortician. It's hard to embalm a body after an autopsy.

"Some of the fellows are pretty good on it. They leave you something to work with, but others go in there and cut arteries and things right and left and it's an awful job embalming."

"Just confidentially," Mason said, "how long before death did Dr. Carver see Gillett?"

"Oh, maybe twenty-four hours."

"And treated him for heart trouble?"

"Well, now, you're asking lots of questions," Bolton said. "As a matter of fact, Doc Carver would see Gillett on the street, maybe at the post office, or someplace like that, and he knew him when he saw him and he'd look him over—you'd be surprised how much a doc can tell about

85

you just by looking at you and the things you do—some of them get so they're pretty goldarned smart."

"I see," Mason said. "So Doctor Carver saw Gorman Gillett at the post office and knew that he would probably be dead within twenty-four hours with a coronary occlusion?"

"Well, now, that's one way of putting it," Bolton said. "Is that the way you *want* to put it?"

"I'd just like to put the way the facts are," Mason said.

"You want the plain truth?"

"That's right."

"Unvarnished?"

"Unvarnished."

"Well," Bolton said, "you're a cash customer, Mr. Mason. You're entitled to service. Now, here's the way the thing was. Gillett had a friend, name of Ezra Honcutt, and he and Ezra were going out, prowling around a little bit— Ezra didn't tell me what they were going to prowl for, but I got a pretty good idea they were going out and spot themselves a little deer meat.

"Anyway, Ezra came up to the cabin and he was going to have breakfast with Gorman, but apparently Gorman wasn't up. There was no sign of activity around the place, no fire, no smell of coffee being on the stove—nothing like that. So Ezra, he just walked in, the way you do up here, and Gorman was lying there in bed, so Ezra said a few things to him about being lazy and stuff like that, and then he saw that Gorman didn't move, so he goes over and gives Gorman a punch in the ribs and then he saw right away Gorman was dead.

"Well, he goes and gets me and I come down and look the thing over and . . . well, you know how it is. I knew old Doc had seen him around, so I went and got Doc and said, 'Doc, you better come take a look.' So Doc came and took a look and said, 'Everything okay?' And I said, 'Everything looks okay to me,' and he pulls back the blankets and we take off Gorman's underwear and there weren't any bullet holes or anything, so Doc says to me, 'Coronary occlusion.' So he says, 'Okay, I'm the attending physician. I'll make out the death certificate, coronary occlusion.'

"So I take Gorman down to my place. Now, that's the sum and substance of the thing. That ain't exactly the way I'd tell it to anybody else, but you being a cash customer, Mr. Mason, you're entitled to the information."

"Thank you," Mason said.

"This man, Gorman, didn't have any relatives," Mason said, "but how about friends—that is, friends from the outside, outside of town?"

"Now, there's something I've been thinking about," Bolton said. "He wasn't particularly sociable. You'll understand when you see the place where he was living.

"He had two or three friends here that he'd go out hunting with, doing a little fishing and . . . well, you know, a little poaching. We're up here in deer country and we don't aim to spend *all* of our money on butcher shops. We aim to be law-abiding but we don't aim to be plumb foolish."

"I understand," Mason said.

"Old Gorman just had one or two old cronies, the same type of fellow he was, but lately—oh, for the past couple of years, someone would drive in to see him once in a while—a good-looking fellow who'd never stop in town, never get acquainted with anybody, just drive right on through to Gorman Gillett's cabin and sit out and visit with him for a while, then jump in his car and beat it."

"Some local speculation about who this person might be?" Mason asked.

"Sure there was. Things go on in this town and people talk about them. You can't help that. People are going to talk about anything that's new and unusual."

"You say this man came up at intervals during the last couple of years?"

"Well, perhaps not just a couple of years, perhaps longer. No one knows exactly when he started coming because no one noticed him at first. But after a while people got to noticing this car would be parked out in front of Gorman's cabin and once the fellow got gas here."

Mason's face showed interest. "Where did he get gas?"

"At that service station there on the corner, right down from my office."

"Do you suppose he used a credit card," Mason asked, "and it would be possible to get the license number or—"

"Nope, I thought of that," Bolton said. "When I was looking for someone to pay the expenses of the funeral I thought of that. But there wasn't any record of the license number.

"Just after you cross this little culvert in the road ahead, you turn to the left and go up a little driveway," Bolton went on. "Take it easy now . . . here's the place. Turn to the left up here."

Mason turned the car and moved slowly up a rather steep driveway.

"I take it," Mason said, "Gorman Gillett didn't have an automobile."

"Automobile!" Bolton said, "Shucks, he didn't even have a toothbrush."

The headlights illuminated a rough cabin.

"I don't know whether Miss Street wants to go in or not," Bolton said. "This fellow was a pretty rough and rugged housekeeper. It's not the type of stuff she's accustomed to."

"She can take it," Mason said. "We want to look around. What are the lighting facilities in there—any electricity?"

"No electricity. He's got a gasoline lantern," Bolton said, "and I've got matches."

They got out of the car onto the spongy carpet of moist pine needles and leaves. Bolton led the way up to the door, fitted the key, unlocked the door, went inside and struck a match.

"Better wait," he said, "until I get this confounded gasoline lantern going."

Della Street sniffed at the stale odor of human occupancy.

"Better take a cigarette, Della," Mason said.

"Thanks, I will."

Mason took a paper package of cigarettes from his pocket. "I miss my silver cigarette case," he said.

"Think you'll ever get it back?"

"Oh, sure," Mason said, "in time. It will have Tragg's initials scratched all over it, just as a souvenir."

Mason held a match to her cigarette, then lit his own. On the inside of the cabin, Bolton could be heard as he pumped up the gasoline lantern, then scraped a match into flame. The gasoline lantern sputtered for a few moments, then the sputtering changed to a hissing sound and the whole interior of the cabin was illuminated with a brilliant white light.

"Come on in, folks," Bolton invited.

The cabin was a one-room affair consisting of a bunk at one end, a table at the other, a stove in between.

A shelf held a few canned goods. There was a sink with two faucets, one for hot and one for cold water, three chairs and a wooden box which had been reinforced so it could serve as an additional chair. On the open shelves were half a dozen dishes, and a cigar box contained a few well-worn knives, forks and some tarnished spoons. On a shelf above the stove was an old battered coffeepot and a teakettle. A washpan was hanging from a nail driven into the wall.

"He lived just sort of simple-like," Bolton explained.

"I see," Mason said.

The lawyer moved over to a corner of the room where some boxes had been nailed together to furnish a sort of storage space in which were piled dozens of dog-eared magazines.

"Any papers?" Mason asked.

"No papers. Not so much as the scratch of a pen—I don't know as he even had a pen to scratch with. There was an old stub of a pencil around here somewhere."

The magazines were pushed into the boxlike receptacle with no attempt at order.

Mason drew up a chair and started to go through them.

"He used to have a fellow that would bring them in from some second-hand magazine store," Bolton explained. "He'd get them when they were sold for a penny apiece."

Mason continued to leaf through the pile. All the stories purported to give the inside dope on true crimes. They fairly reeked murder.

Bolton, interpreting Mason's thougths, said, "That was all he went for. Me, I like detective fiction. My wife likes travel. That's the way it goes—everybody to his taste. Gillett liked murder."

Mason said, "Here's one that's different."

The lawyer pulled out a copy of the *Saturday Evening Post* dated some two and a half years eari-lier.

"That's right," Bolton said. "I seen that when I was up here taking inventory. That's the only regular one he had in the place."

Mason glanced through the magazine, suddenly stopped, then, noticing Bolton's eyes on him, turned the pages casually to the end and tossed the magazine to one side. "What else?" he asked. "You said he lived on jerky?"

"Quite a bit."

"What did he kill the deer with?"

Bolton said, "You *would* ask that."

"Have a gun?" Mason inquired.

Bolton said, "Yep. He had a very fine gun and he sure kept that gun oiled and shined. There wasn't a speck of rust or dust on it."

"Where's the gun?" Mason asked.

"I got it over at my place for safekeeping," Bolton said. "It's a pretty good gun. You can't tell what might happen to it—I figured I could get my undertaking fees out of that if I had to."

"Well," Mason said, "if there aren't any heirs, it *should* be held by you, shouldn't it?"

"You know, Mr. Mason," Bolton said, "you're a pretty darn good lawyer. You have the right type of thinking. You sure got what they call a legal mind. I bet you, you could come up here and get a cabin and fit right in with the people around here."

"It's an interesting thought," Mason said. "Sometime when I get a little more time I might like to have a cabin where I could spend week ends and vacations."

"Best country on earth," Bolton said. "People come up here with one foot in the grave and keep on living and living and living . . . dammit, I guess I ought to know. I've been cheated out of more fees by people getting well up here than I'd care to tell you about— Anything else you want to see around here?"

"I don't think so," Mason said. "I presume you've been through the stuff."

"Such as it is, I've been through it," Bolton said. "When I've got a corpse and there isn't any money to bury him with, I look around right sharp."

"He didn't have any money?" Mason asked.

"Had about seventeen dollars in cash in that old coffee can up there, and that was it."

"No letters, no post cards, nothing that would indicate anyone wrote to him or took an interest in him?"

"Nothing at all."

Mason said, "I want to go out to my car and get my brief case before we leave here. There's one thing I'd like to show you."

"Okay," Bolton said. "We could all go out to the car and—"

"No," Mason said. "This gasoline lantern gives a pretty good light and you may need a good light."

"I'll get the brief case," Della Street said, and hurried out of the cabin to return in a moment with Mason's brief case.

"Now," Mason said, "you mentioned the young man who came up to see Gorman Gillett on occasion. I believe you said you'd seen him?"

"Sure, I've seen him."

"Would you know him if you saw him again?"

"Think so."

"Would you be able to recognize his photograph?"

"Now, that's different," Bolton said. "It depends on the photograph a lot. I've seen some people that took pictures you could recognize right away, and I've seen some people that didn't—maybe it's the people, maybe it's the picture, I don't know."

Mason took the photograph of Frankline Gillett from the brief case and handed it to Bolton.

Bolton regarded the photograph thoughtfully, then took it over close to the gasoline lantern and held it so the bright rays were falling directly on the picture.

"It's hard to say," he said, "because there aren't any colors here and, to my mind, colors have a lot to do with an identification. But, you know, Mr. Mason, I've got me an idea this here's the fellow."

"Well," Mason said, "I'd like to be sure, but—"

"Well, it sure looks like him," Bolton said. "Now, look, Hy Lovell is down here at the service station. He'll be there until eleven-thirty. He got a pretty good look at the fellow and he was kind of curious, and then there's Ezra Honcutt, who discovered the body. He lives up here about a mile up the road."

"Could we see him?" Mason asked.

"Shucks, he's gone to bed now," Bolton said, "but if you want to see him, we can see him."

"I want to see him."

"Let's go," Bolton said.

They extinguished the gasoline lantern, Bolton locked up the cabin and Mason drove the car up the road until he brought it to a stop in front of a cabin indicated by Bolton.

Bolton said, "Better let me get him up. People around here get kinda suspicious of strangers sometimes, particularly when they show up at night."

Bolton got out of the car, advanced a few feet, raised his voice and called out, "Hi, Ezra."

Almost instantly a dry, cackling voice from the interior of the cabin said, "That you, Manny?"

"That's me," Bolton said.

"What you want?"

"Want to talk."

"Who's with you?"

"A man and a young woman."

"Who are they?"

"Fellow from the city."

"Don't want to talk."

"You'll want to talk with this fellow. He's all right. And this woman that's with him is mighty pert."

"Got my long handles on," Ezra said.

"Well, pull on your Levis over your long handles," Bolton told him. "Put down that there shooting iron you're holding and get a light on in your cabin and get dressed up."

"Who told you I was holding a shooting iron?"

Bolton snorted. "I wasn't born yesterday and I ain't gonna die tomorrow. Bet you came out of your bunk and your feet hit the floor and your hand grabbed the gun within half a second of the time we turned off the road and you saw the headlights in the window of your cabin. Now quit being so goldanged coy and get your clothes on and get that door open."

"Okay, okay," the dry voice cackled. "Give a man time, can't you?"

Mason and Della Street sat in the automobile while

Bolton stood impatiently waiting outside until a light came on in the cabin. Then Bolton walked up and pushed open the door. "I'll call you folks in a minute," he said.

Bolton was inside the cabin for nearly a minute, then he came to the door and said, "Okay, he's decent now, got his Levis on."

Mason and Della Street left the automobile and entered the cabin.

This was another one-roomed cabin but a little more neat than the Gillett cabin.

Ezra Honcutt proved to be a tall, cadaverous individual, attired only in a red woolen union suit of underwear and overalls. The upper portion of the underwear, which originally had been a cherry red, had been faded by much use, and was slightly drab. Big feet with enlarged joints at the big toes were bare.

Here again, a bunk was at one end of the cabin and blankets had been hastily thrown back. There were no sheets on the bed; a pillow had a somewhat grimy Turkish towel thrown over it for a pillowcase.

A deer-hunting rifle stood in a corner by the bed, and hanging from a wooden peg was a six-shooter and a belt full of cartridges.

"This here's Ezra Honcutt," Bolton said. "That's Perry Mason and the young woman with him is named Street."

Ezra Honcutt looked up somewhat furtively. He was somewhere in his sixties, with a bony frame, a long, slim neck, a protruding Adam's apple and a shock of unkempt hair.

He stretched a hand across the table and gripped Mason's fingers. "Glad to know you," he said.

He looked at Della Street and bowed bashfully.

"I got a coat around here somewhere," he said to Della Street. "Didn't know you were quite so pert or I'd have had it on."

"Never mind," Bolton said. "You're decent and that's

enough . . . This man here has a picture he wants you to look at."

"What king of picture?" Ezra Honcutt asked.

"Picture of a feller." Bolton said.

"Okay, I'll look."

Mason took the photograph from the brief case, handed it to Honcutt.

"Ever see this feller before, Ezra?" Bolton asked.

Ezra studied the picture, then slowly handed it back, thought for a moment, took a plug of tobacco from his pants pocket, cut off a piece and put it in his mouth.

"Know him?" Bolton asked.

"Ain't sure," Honcutt said.

"What do you think?"

"Think I do."

"Who?"

"Feller come up here a couple of times to see Gorman."

"That's what I thought," Bolton said. "You don't know his name?"

"Nope."

"Never talked with him?"

"Nope."

"All we wanted to know," Bolton said. "We're leaving. Sorry we had to get you up, but this feller is in a hurry. He's gotta get clean back to the big city tonight."

Ezra's pale blue eyes searched Mason's face.

Bolton chuckled.

"What's the matter?" Ezra asked.

"Think you know him?" Bolton asked.

"Something familiar about him," Honcutt said.

Bolton chuckled.

"Well, ain't you going to tell me?"

"Tell you what?"

"What's familiar about him."

"If I have to tell you, he ain't that familiar."

"All right, he ain't that familiar."

"You'll be seeing him again," Bolton said. "Well, so long."

Ezra Honcutt raised hurt eyes. "You ain't going to tell me?"

"I ain't going to tell you nothing," Bolton said. "We're on our way."

Ezra arose from the creaking wooden chair to stand at his full height, a height that was considerably above six feet. He pushed forward a long, bony arm, and gnarled knuckles once more enveloped Mason's hand.

"Pleasure," he said.

"It was a pleasure to me," Mason said, "and thanks a lot for your help."

Ezra Honcutt shifted his eyes to Della Street, promptly lowered them to the floor. "Good night, ma'am," he said.

"Good night," Della Street said, "and I'm very pleased I met you and thanks a lot for your help."

She moved impulsively toward him and extended her hand.

Honcutt's Adam's apple raced up and down his throat twice before he could say, "Thank you, ma'am, very much."

For a moment he touched her hand, then pulled his own hand back.

"Be seeing you," Bolton said, and led the way out the cabin door.

"Want to talk with Hy Lovell at the service station?" Bolton asked.

Mason nodded.

"Okay, we'll drive there."

They drove along the slippery road, dodging the numerous puddles of muddy water, back to Pine Haven.

Mason drove his car into the service station. "Fill 'er up," he said.

The young man looked curiously at Mason, lingeringly at Della Street, said nothing.

Bolton said, "Hy, this man's got a couple of questions he wants to ask you."

"Okay."

"Wants you to take a look at a picture."

"Okay."

Mason got out of the car and the others followed.

Mason again opened the brief case, took out the picture, showed it to Lovell.

"Seen this feller before?" Bolton asked.

Lovell held the gasoline hose with his left hand, made no effort to touch the picture but leaned over to study it for nearly five seconds, then straightened back to give his undivided attention to the stream of gasoline pouring into the tank.

"Well?" Bolton asked.

"Yep." Lovell said.

"Where?"

"He's the feller that came here for gas, called on Gorman Gillett a couple of times."

"Thanks," Bolton said.

Mason put the picture back in the brief case. Lovell put the cap on the gas tank, tested the oil and water, washed the windshield and said, "Three-eighty-five," to Mason.

The lawyer handed him a five-dollar bill, said, "I haven't got time to wait for change. I'm in something of a hurry. Thanks a lot."

The lawyer jumped in the car. Della Street climbed into the middle of the front seat, and Bolton seated himself beside her.

Mason drove out.

"Well, I guess that's him," Bolton said.

"Seems like it," Mason said.

"You can drop me off at my place," Bolton said.

Mason stopped the car at the Bolton Funeral Home.

"Well, good night," Bolton said.

"Thanks a lot to you," Mason said.

"Thanks a lot to you," Bolton retorted.

Mason said, "You haven't asked me who the young fellow is."

"That's right, I haven't," Bolton said. "Figured if you wanted to tell me, you would, and if you didn't, you wouldn't. You're a cash customer."

Mason said, "I think you'll see this face in the papers tomorrow. Confidentially, I have reason to believe he was Gorman Gillett's son, but I wouldn't want you to say anything about it until I'm sure."

Bolton shook his head. "If you don't want me to say anything about something, don't tell me," he said. "You tell me and I'll talk."

"All right," Mason said, grinning. "I've told you."

"I'll talk," Bolton said. "Up here, the guy that's first with something like that is important."

"All right," Mason told him, "you can get important tomorrow."

"Tomorrow, hell," Bolton said. "I'm going to walk right back down to that service station."

The mortician waved to them as the lawyer drove off along the paved highway.

"Well?" Della Street asked.

"It certainly seems that death didn't waste any time once it got started with the Gillett family," Mason said.

"Do you suppose the grandchild is all right, Perry?"

"I don't know," Mason said. And then added, "We'll try to find out."

"Why did you tell him, Perry?" Della Street asked.

"Tell him what?"

"About Frankline Gillett being the son of Gorman Gillett."

"He'd been frank with me," Mason said, "and I thought I should be frank with him, particularly since he'll recognize the picture when he sees it in the city papers—and you notice he had the metropolitan newspapers on his desk."

"All right," Della said, "quit being mysterious. What was in the *Saturday Evening Post*?"

"What made you think something was in it?"

"You glanced through it, stopped, looked up, saw Bolton watching you, and then thumbed the pages so casually that I knew you'd struck pay dirt."

"Was I that obvious?" Mason asked.

"To me, you were. What was the article?"

"The article," Mason said, "was about a businessman who made a fortune buying up old adobe houses, fixing them up so as to preserve the old atmosphere but giving them modern conveniences, and selling them at a whale of a profit. The name, in case you're interested, was . . ."

Della Street chimed in so that her voice blended with Mason's. "George Belding Baxter," they both said together.

Mason grinned. Della Street laughed.

"Still one jump ahead of the police," Mason said. "Now we'll go give these fingerprints to Paul Drake and see what we draw."

# Chapter 11

Mason latchkeyed the door to his private office, tossed the morning newspaper on the desk, said, "Hi, Della, how long have you been here?"

"Fifteen or twenty minutes."

"Heard anything from Paul Drake?"

"He says he has a whole bunch of stuff and wants you to call him as soon as you come in."

"How's he feeling?"

"Lousy," she said. "He was up most of the night and got indigestion from drinking lots of coffee and he says the hamburgers all soured on his stomach. He says he's had so much bicarbonate of soda he feels like a biscuit."

"Good old Paul," Mason said. "Back to normal. Tell him I'm here, Della. Ask him to come in and we'll see what he has."

Della Street gave Paul a ring, and within almost a matter of seconds Drake was tapping his code knock on the door of the private office.

Della Street opened the door. Drake focused haggard eyes on Perry Mason and said, "You sure raised hell up at Pine Haven."

"What happened?" Mason asked.

"Lieutenant Tragg's gone boiling up there."

"Trying to find a clue?" Mason asked.

"Trying to find what *you've* been up to," Drake said.

Mason grinned. "As long as I can keep him running around behind me that way, I'm fixed. What did you do with those fingerprints I left in your office last night?"

"Whose were they?" Drake asked.

Mason shook his head. "Naughty, naughty, Paul. You mustn't ask questions where the answers would give you knowledge that would embarrass you."

"Well, I called in a fingerprint expert," Drake said, "got him to classify the prints, and we got a friendly chief of police in one of the outlying towns to wire in to the FBI after we got the classification."

"Heard anything yet?"

"Not yet, but we should have it any minute—that is, if there's a record. . . . Tell me, Perry, those fingerprints weren't . . ."

Drake's voice trailed off into silence.

"Yes?" Mason prompted.

"I don't think I want to know the answer," Drake said. "Now, here's something you should know. The police traced the gun, all right. Actually, they didn't have to. It was purchased by George Belding Baxter and given to his housekeeper about two weeks ago."

"Who's the housekeeper?"

"Minnie Crowder."

"And it was her night off when the murder was committed?"

"That's right."

"All right, what did she do with the gun?"

Drake said, "Baxter gave her the gun about two weeks ago. About eight or nine days ago she lost it out of her coat pocket. She was afraid to tell Baxter because he had stalled about giving her a gun, telling her that she'd be careless and lose it and it would be registered in his name and someone would commit a crime with it, and all of that."

"All right, what happened?"

"No one knows. The gun fell out of her pocket while she was taking a walk and carrying her coat over her arm."

"Was it the murder weapon?" Mason asked.

"They haven't released any information on that, but the chances are a hundred to one it was.

"George Belding Baxter said he only bought the one gun and that was the one he gave to the housekeeper for protection."

Mason said, "Paul, I'm going to get this thing set down for a hearing. I'm going to have subpoenas issued. I want you to serve a subpoena on George Belding Baxter to appear as a witness for the defense."

"You can't do that."

"Why not?"

"My gosh, Perry, have a heart! George Belding Baxter is a multimillionaire, he's got interests all over the country, he's all set to take off for Honolulu."

"He'll remain here after I serve him with a subpoena," Mason said.

"He'll raise the roof," Drake warned.

"Put a man on him right now," Mason said. "I want him kept under surveillance so that when it comes time to serve the subpoena we'll know where he is. Don't let him know that he's being shadowed, just keep a line on him so we can serve him with a subpoena, and I also want a subpoena served on Minnie Crowder the housekeeper. And what's that caretaker's name out there?"

"Corley Ketchum."

"Okay," Mason said, "we're going to serve all of them with subpoenas. What's the police theory, Paul?"

"Heaven knows by this time," Drake said. "They did have the idea that Gillett and Gwynn Elston had got together, that they were having a down-to-earth talk, that for some reason they turned in at the grounds at the Baxter place and she shot him. They think there probably was someone else with her."

"That was the original theory," Mason said. "Are they holding to it now?"

"I don't know," Drake said. "If Gwynn Elston would tell any kind of a convincing story, I think they'd turn her loose for the time being."

"Only to drag her back in front of a grand jury later on," Mason said.

"Her complete refusal to talk, to answer any questions at all, has put her behind the eight ball as far as publicity is concerned, Perry. Everybody thinks she's guilty or she wouldn't be keeping silent."

"I don't give a damn what everybody thinks," Mason said. "It's what the jury is going to think that counts. Now, what about that man who parked the car out at the gates of the Baxter estate—"

Drake interrupted him with a shake of his head. "I keep telling you, Perry, there wasn't any such man. There *was* a man who was with Gwynn Elston when she drove up to the service station. The man asked the attendant something about the rest room and then walked around the station on the wrong side. The attendant didn't try to stop him. Sometimes people get directions mixed up and walk around, but they always find the place they're looking for in the long run—the only thing is, this fellow just walked around the station and as soon as he got on the dark side of the station he took off."

"Leaving Gwynn Elston with a hot gun," Mason said.

"That's her claim," Drake said. "Do you believe it in view of all the other evidence?"

"I don't know," Mason said.

"Well, if you believe it, you'll be about the only one that does," Drake told him.

"Then it's up to me to handle the problem of public relations so certain other people believe it too."

"What people?"

"Prospective jurors."

"How do you propose to do that?"

"You furnish me with facts, Paul, and I'll stir them in with a little theory and we may be able to bake a cake."

"Be careful you don't get your fingers burned," Drake warned.

"I'll keep your warning in mind."

"I'm going to be mighty careful with my own fingers," Drake said.

"Okay," Mason said, "get busy. Get your men out on Baxter so we know where he is all the time and . . ."

The lawyer broke off as the telephone bell rang.

Della street picked up the receiver, motioned to Paul and said, "Your office, Paul."

Drake got on the line, said, "Hello . . . yeah . . . let me get that again. . . . Okay, what's the name? . . . Write this down, will you, Della? How do you spell it? . . . Oh, heck, we know all about him," Drake said.

He was silent for a moment, said, "Are you sure? Well, that's a funny thing. Who was the other guy? . . . Collington Halsey?"

"That's H-a-l-s-e-y? Right . . . now, what's that first name again? . . . C-o-l-l-i-n-g-t-o-n? . . . Collington? . . . Right.

"And where was this? . . . When was it? . . . Okay. Yeah, I've got it. . . . No attempt at changing a name, eh? . . . Okay."

Drake hung up the telephone, said to Mason, "Those fingerprints were Gorman Gillett's. He served time in Fort Madison, Iowa, for armed robbery—seven years."

"How long ago?"

"Twenty years ago."

"What's the other name?" Mason asked.

"That was the accomplice that was with him, a fellow by the name of Collington Halsey. Halsey and Gillett escaped. The officers nabbed Gillett but they never did catch up with Halsey. . . . The FBI got a little excited when the chief of police sent in Gillett's fingerprints. They want to know all about where he is, because they think perhaps he may know where Halsey is. They want to question Halsey about a murder."

"If he knows where Halsey is now," Mason said, "he's going to keep the information to himself. He . . ."

"Okay," Drake said. "What struck you, Perry?"

"An idea," Mason said.

"I gathered as much," Drake told him. "Anything you care to pass on?"

Mason said, "It's just a hunch, a wild-eyed hunch."

"Want to tell it to me?"

Mason shook his head. "Go get your men out and keep Baxter under surveillance until I can get a subpoena. Get started."

"The FBI is all excited about Gorman Gillett," Drake said.

"Tell them to send a floral piece to the funeral, Paul."

"This officer who sent in the prints for me says the FBI is after him to give him what information he has."

Mason said, "The FBI will have it by noon. The first thing Tragg and that outfit will do will be to take Gillett's fingerprints just in case."

"And why did *you* take them?" Drake asked.

"Just in case," Mason said. "Get started, Paul."

After Drake had left the office, Della Street said to Perry Mason, "Could I make a guess as to what your idea was?"

"You could," Mason said.

"George Belding Baxter?" she asked.

Mason nodded. "It's a wild idea," he said, "but let's begin to put two and two together and see how much we can make. Gorman Gillett was a buddy of Collington Halsey. They pulled a stick-up. Gillett served time, Halsey escaped. They never found a trace of him. Now, what does that mean?"

"You tell me," Della said.

Mason said, "It means that Halsey got some kind of a completely fresh start and got out of the underworld and away from a life of crime. He got in a position where no one would ever dare suspect him."

"How do you deduce that?"

"Because they had his fingerprints on file and they've never seen them again," Mason said. "You take anyone who's on the fringes of a criminal life and sooner or later the police get his fingerprints."

"They haven't taken mine—that is, recently," Della Street said.

"You're not on the fringes of a criminal life," Mason said. "Even so, you get your fingerprints taken once in a while. But anyone who's wandering around mixed up with a criminal element is going to get picked up on suspicion of this or that, and they'll take his fingerprints. They come in to the FBI at intervals whenever a wanted man is at liberty. Now, Halsey vanished into thin air."

"Go on," Della Street said.

"Gillett served his time, decided to hell with all that criminal stuff, went up to a little town, got himself a cabin, did a little prospecting, lived on venison and trout with a little flour and bacon once in a while, and then one day, two and a half years ago, picked up a *Saturday Evening Post* and saw photographs of George Belding Baxter, the multimillionaire.

"Now, let's just suppose that he recognized the photographs as being of Collington Halsey. What do you suppose happened after that?"

"Do you suppose Gillett got in touch with George Belding Baxter?" she asked.

"Why not?"

"He doesn't seem to have made much out of it."

"He didn't want much out of it," Mason said. "All he wanted by that time was a sack of flour, a little bacon, some coffee and some salt. He was happy."

"And then?"

"Then," Mason said, "his son found him. His son wasn't particularly proud of Father, but he looked the old man up anyway. Then he began to wonder how Father was supporting himself, and he became rather solicitous as a son, wondering just where the money came from."

"Now," Della Street said, "you fascinate me."

"It's a fascinating situation," Mason said. "The son found out that Baxter was Collington Halsey, and the son started leading a double life. He committed bigamy; he gravitated from one place to the other; he had a mysterious business; no one knows anything about it; he didn't make joint income tax returns; he began to live on the fat of the land."

"And then?" Della Street prompted.

"And then," Mason said, "All of a sudden death took a hand. Both father and son died within forty-eight hours of each other. And Baxter gets in a great hurry to get out of the country so in case anyone thinks about taking the finger-prints of the people in the Baxter household to see if they are unaccounted for, no one will be in a position to say, 'Now, Mr. Baxter, if you don't mind, we'd like to have your fingerprints, just for purposes of comparison.'"

"And you're about to serve a subpoena on George Belding Baxter," Della Street said.

Mason grinned.

"What a spot *you're* in," Della Street said. "Baxter will—Chief, do you suppose you might meet with . . . ?"

"With what?" Mason asked.

"With coronary occlusion?" she asked.

Mason laughed. "I'll stay away from Dr. Ewald Carver, and if I show up missing, be sure there's an autopsy, Della. . . . Dammit, why didn't I have the presence of mind to steal that *Saturday Evening Post* out of the Gillett cabin?"

Della Street said, "Do you suppose Tragg is there yet?"

"He'll be getting there any time now," Mason said. "As soon as he sees that one *Saturday Evening Post* in the midst of all those true crime magazines, Lieutenant Tragg will be right up with us in his thinking."

"That will be bad?" Della Street asked.

"It will rob us of our lead. I'm sorry about that *Post* being left there."

"Do you dare to take it now?" she asked.

"Heavens, no. That might be removing evidence. We couldn't do that."

"Well, what could we do?"

"We might make it somewhat less conspicuous," Mason said, frowning thoughtfully.

"Well," she told him, "you're a cash customer."

A slow smile spread over Mason's face. "Get Manny G. Bolton up at the Bolton Funeral Home in Pine Haven, Della."

Della Street put through the call. A few moments later, she nodded to Perry Mason.

Mason picked up the telephone, said, "Good morning, Mr. Bolton. How's everything this morning?"

"Coming fine," Bolton said, "just fine."

"And news up at your end?"

"Not a thing. No more than there was there last night."

Mason said, "You know, I've been thinking about poor old Gorman up there."

"Yeah, what about him?"

Mason said, "You know and I know how those things are, Bolton. We realize that when a person is lonely and gets to reading, he's apt to do a certain type of reading."

"Yeah, go ahead," Bolton said. "What's on your mind?"

"I wouldn't want people to think that my relative didn't read anything except crime magazines, even if he is only a distant relative."

"So what?" Bolton asked. "Just tell me what you want, Mr. Mason. You're a cash customer."

"Oh," Mason said, "I thought that it might look bad if word got out that there was nothing there in the cabin except those magazines and—"

"You want me to go down and get them and then burn 'em up?" Bolton asked.

"Oh, not that," Mason said, "but . . . *you* must have a bunch of old magazines around your place, haven't you? You said your wife was interested in travel?"

"That's right, got stacks of 'em. Got a whole woodshed full."

"How about taking three or four dozen different types of magazines down there and putting them in with the crime stories?"

"But not taking out any of the crime stories?"

"Oh, no," Mason said. "I don't think there's any necessity to take anything *out*. We just make it appear that Uncle Gorman was a little more varied in his reading."

"Uncle Gorman, eh?"

"I was just calling him that," Mason said.

"I understand, Mr. Mason. I'll take 'em right now."

"Right away?"

"Right now."

"And, of course," Mason said, "there's no need to remember just what magazines you take down there."

"Now, don't worry a bit," Bolton said. "You know, Mr. Mason, I think you'd get along fine up here in this community. I think people would like you. I think you'd get along and you probably wouldn't have too big a meat bill living up this way."

"It's a fascinating thought," Mason said.

"Well," Bolton told him, "I want you to know we always appreciate people that are understanding."

"That's fine," Mason said. "I'll be seeing you one of these days." And he hung up.

Della Street watched him with apprehensive eyes. "Is there any crime connected with this?" she asked.

"Connected with what?"

"Planting evidence."

"Evidence of what?"

"Evidence that would . . . well, you know."

Mason said, "I don't know of any statute that says it's a crime to put old reading matter in the cabin of a man who died of coronary occlusion. Remember, there's a doctor's certificate stating the cause of death. No foul play there."

"But how about planting false evidence? Isn't there something—"

"Evidence of what?" Mason asked. "And what's false about it?"

"Well, you're making it so that one issue of the *Saturday Evening Post* in that cabin doesn't stand out quite so prominently."

"And that's a crime?" Mason asked.

"I don't know," she said, "I'm just wondering."

Mason winked. "We're keeping one jump ahead of the police, Della, and it's a grand and glorious sensation. Usually we're one jump behind and they won't give us the time of day."

"But suppose Bolton tells them he took down a lot of other magazines at your request?"

"Because I didn't want it to appear there was nothing in the place except crime magazines," Mason said. "Now, if Bolton remembers each and every magazine he took down there, that might help. But if he should state that there was nothing in the place except the so-called true crime stories and he took down a bunch of family magazines to put in there, Tragg will assume all the magazines other than the crime magazines were taken down there as red herrings, and he'll read and reread the crime magazines, searching for the particular issue I was trying to cover up."

Della Street sighed and said, "Well, you're the cash customer."

"I am for a fact," Mason said. "And right now we've got to get the fingerprints of Collington Halsey and then we're going to have to make some reasonable excuse so we can get at least one fingerprint of George Belding Baxter."

"Such as having an automobile accident and inspecting his driving license?" Della Street asked.

"That might do it," Mason said, "but he might be just a little suspicious. I'd like to get some of his fingerprints when he didn't know he was giving them to me."

"And just how are we going to work that?"

Mason said, "I wish I had my cigarette case back. Della, go down to the jewelry store, get some polished silver cigarette cases and two fine desk lighters and then wipe them all off clean as a whistle with a chamois skin."

"And then?" she asked.

"Then we leave them sitting around the waiting room in the office and we put a duplicate set on the desk in here."

"And you think George Belding Baxter is coming to you?"

"He's coming to me," Mason said. "After I serve him with that subpoena, which we should be able to do by noon, George Belding Baxter is going to come in here so fast that he's apt to take the door right off the hinges."

"And while he's here, he'll leave fingerprints?"

Mason nodded.

Della Street said, "You're one jump ahead of the police, all right, but it is anyone's guess which way you're jumping and I hope you can see what's underneath when you come down. . . . How strong do you want me to go on the silverware?"

"Get whatever's necessary," Mason said. "I want it to look tempting and inviting, and get a chamois skin and make sure there isn't a fingerprint on any of the articles when you put them out in the office. . . . Ain't we got fun!"

"We've got something," Della Street said, "but heaven knows what it's going to be. Let's hope it's fun."

# Chapter 12

It was three-twenty-five in the afternoon when the receptionist rang three short rings, the agreed upon signal.

Perry Mason smiled. "That," he said to Della Street, "means that the quarry has walked into our trap. George Belding Baxter is in the outer office. Go out and tell him that I am occupied at the moment but that I will try and see him. Ask him to be seated for a few minutes. Be sure that you put him in the seat that is next to the silver cigarette case and the lighter. Tell Gertie to ring twice as soon as he's picked up the objects."

Della Street said, "Check. We've rehearsed it a couple of times. You can count on Gertie for something like that. She loves intrigue."

Della Street went out to the outer office, was gone a couple of minutes, came back and said to Perry Mason, "Boy, is *he* hopping mad! I had the darnedest time trying to get him to sit down. He wanted to pace the office, and I thought for a minute he was going to just push his way through the door and come in."

"But he's seated now?"

"He's seated."

"Nervous?"

"Nervous, angry and . . . and just plain mad."

"Well," Mason said, "if he's nervous, he won't be able to keep his hands off those nice shiny objects and . . ."

The phone rang two short rings.

Mason grinned, said, "That means he's left his fingerprints. Go out and bring him in, Della, then tell Gertie to slide some cardboard under the cigarette case and the lighter, lift them up and give Paul Drake the signal. That will give Paul something to work on."

Della Street nodded, left the office and a few moments later returned with a big man in his fifties, a man who pushed past her as soon as the door was opened and said, "Mason, I'm George Belding Baxter. What the hell's the idea of serving this paper on me?"

Baxter whipped a paper from his pocket and slammed it down on the desk.

Mason arose from his chair, stood smiling, said, "All right, Baxter, my name's Mason. What the hell's the idea of storming into my office this way?"

"Because I'm mad."

"All right," Mason said, "if you want to stay mad, storm your way out again. If you want to sit down and talk, sit down in that chair and talk."

Baxter said, "I'm *going* to talk!"

"Then sit down."

"*I* can say what *I* have to say standing up."

"All right," Mason said, "*I* can listen standing up. You've been served with a subpoena. I want you to testify for the defense."

"I don't know a damn thing about the case."

Mason sat down at his desk, pulled some papers over to him and started reading. He might not have heard Baxter's remark, if his actions were any indication.

Baxter stood irresolute for a moment, then walked over to the desk. "You can't get away with this, do you hear?"

Mason didn't look up.

Baxter nervously fingered the cigarette lighter on the desk as if he might be planning to use it as a weapon.

Mason went right on reading.

Baxter said, "I'm going to Honolulu."

"That's fine," Mason said.

"Tonight."

"Then you'll have to be back in time for the preliminary hearing," Mason said.

"Just what the devil are you trying to do?" Baxter demanded. "I don't know anything that would be of any value to you or your client. I don't know the defendant, Gwynn Elston. I didn't know the man who was murdered. I don't know a thing about the case. I was away at the time. The murder happened to take place on the grounds near my house, that's all I know. I only know that because someone told me."

"What about the gun?"

"I bought it, there's no question about that."

"Then you can testify to that."

"I don't have to, the records speak for themselves. There's no question about who bought the gun. I signed for it on the firearms sales register."

"That makes it very interesting," Mason said.

Baxter said, "Look, I came here to tell you that I simply can't postpone my trip to Honolulu."

"Then come back for the hearing."

"I can't. I can't go over and then turn around and come right back."

"Then stay here."

"Look here, Mason," Baxter said, "I've tried to be nice to you. I've tried to make it easy for you. Now, if you want to do it the hard way, we'll do it the hard way.

"I have a battery of attorneys. They know all the law you do, and perhaps a little you've never heard of. You have, for some reason of your own, used the process of the court in order to subpoena me, simply for the purpose of inconveniencing me, not for the purpose of getting any information out of me. There's some form of legal blackmail connected with this. My attorneys instructed me to explain the circumstances to you and request that you excuse me from attendance at the trial. I'm following their instructions."

Mason said, "You've explained the circumstances. I haven't excused you."

Baxter said, "All right, Mason. My attorneys anticipated that. I've done what they told me to. Now I'll make them earn their fees."

He turned and strode from the office.

Mason picked up the telephone, said, "Did you get Paul, Gertie?"

"Yes, he's out here in the office now with his fingerprint man."

"Tell him to come in here as soon as he's done," Mason said. "We have some more prints."

A few moments later, Della Street and Drake, accompanied by a slender, nervous individual, entered the room.

Drake said, "Mason, shake hands with Stan Doyle. He's one of the best fingerprint men I know— You have some latents here?"

Mason shook hands and said, "We should have some good ones." He indicated the big lighter on the desk.

Doyle inspected the cigarette lighter, then took a small bottle and a brush from his pocket. He brushed dust over the gleaming surface.

Fingerprints showed immediately with startling visibility.

"I'll say. You've got some good ones," he said.

"What do we do now?" Mason asked.

"We take these objects down to Drake's office and photograph them."

"And then what?"

"We have the fingerprints of Mr. X from the FBI," Drake said, "and we can tell you within ten minutes whether or not your man is Mr. X."

Mason said, "That's what I want. I want to be sure. And I want proof."

"We can probably do even better than that," Doyle went on. "I think we have enough fingerprints here so we can

116

combine them with what we secured from the outer office and make a classification."

"All right," Mason said, "What we want is speed, because I have an idea the man who just called on me isn't going to let any grass grow under his feet."

Doyle put cardboard under the cigarette lighter and the cigarette case, said, "All right, Paul, we'll go down to your office and get to work. . . . I could save time if I could lift these fingerprints, Mr. Mason, instead of photographing them."

"No," Mason said, "then we'd lose the advantage of having the fingerprints in place. Just develop your photographs and then compare them with the prints of Mr. X that Paul Drake has, and let me know."

When they had left the office, Della Street said, "What would happen if it should be a mistake, Perry?"

"Plenty," Mason said, grinning. "We're gambling, but I think we're gambling on a sure thing. The whole history of this case just fits together into a pattern."

"It does for a fact," Della Street said. "Only . . . it's circumstantial evidence."

"It's circumstantial evidence," Mason said, "which is some of the best evidence we have—although that's not always the way we talk to a jury."

Mason was in high good humor.

The phone rang, and Della Street picked up the phone, said, "Yes, Gertie?" Then turned to Mason, "Your man, Baxter, works fast. There's a process server out here wanting to serve you with papers."

"Tell him to come right in," Mason said. "We're always glad to be served with papers."

Della Street went out and ushered in the process server. "Thank you for seeing me, Mr. Mason," the man said. "So many people try to take things out on a process server. After all, I'm just paid to hand you papers."

"Go ahead and hand them," Mason said. "What are they?"

"George Belding Baxter's motion to quash a subpoena, and a civil suit for damages against you for a hundred thousand dollars, claiming that you deliberately abused the process of the court in order to interfere with his business and cause him a lot of inconvenience."

"Well," Mason said, "when Baxter does something, he really does it. I suppose he had you waiting down at the entrance to the building?"

"Well," the process server said, "I believe I was held in escrow, so to speak. I was waiting by the elevators."

Mason said, "All right, you've served me. That's fine."

The process server went out, and Mason looked over the papers.

"When Baxter fights, he really fights," he said. "This suit for a hundred thousand dollars is designed to frighten me and put me on the defensive—wait until *we* lower the boom on *him*."

Ten minutes later the unlisted telephone rang.

"That'll be Paul," Mason said. "He's a little ahead of time."

Mason himself scooped up the receiver, said, "Yes, Paul?"

Paul Drake's voice, sharp with worry, came over the line. "Look, Perry, before we photographed those prints we did a little work with a magnifying glass, and I can tell you right now that you're barking up the wrong tree. George Belding Baxter is *not* Collington Halsey."

Mason sat for a moment and digested that information.

"You got that?" Drake asked.

"I got it," Mason said, "right between the eyes. Get your man to work on the classification of the fingerprints. If he isn't Halsey, let's find out who the hell he really is."

Mason hung up the telephone.

Della Street said, her voice showing alarm, "It didn't pan out?"

Mason shook his head. "Not yet."

"Where does that leave you, Chief?" Della Street asked.

"Very much behind the eight ball," Mason said. "Hang it, Della, I *can't* be wrong! Too many things point to it, and yet . . . yet it seems I *am* wrong, unless that man's managed to have new fingerprints grafted on his fingers, and they tell me that's impossible."

"When you stop to think of it," Della Street said, "he did seem to walk into our trap most beautifully. He handled everything *so* obligingly.

Mason frowned. "I wonder if— My gosh, Della, do you suppose he was smart enough to figure out what I wanted him to do, and all the time was chuckling to himself, thinking about the foundation for a beautiful lawsuit he was building up?"

"*I'm* not making any guesses," Della Street said.

Mason smiled ruefully. "It does look like we'd used up our allowance of wild ones for the day."

# Chapter 13

Mason and Della Street, returning from dinner, stopped in at Paul Drake's office.

"Well, what's the bad news by this time?" Mason asked.

"Lots of it," Drake said. "We managed to get enough prints from those silver articles to give us a complete classification. We wired the FBI and got a reply. George Belding Baxter is as clean as a hound's tooth. He's never had his fingerprints taken. He's George Belding Baxter, and that's all."

Mason digested that bit of information in thoughtful silence.

"Moreover," Drake went on, "the newspapers have made a big thing about the suit he filed against you. Baxter has given a couple of interviews in which he stated that he'll spend a million dollars, if necessary, in order to show you that you can't use the subpoena of a court to obtain some personal advantage, that you are trying to inconvenience him, that he has no information that would be of any value in connection with the case against your client, and that he has suffered heavy damages because he can't leave on his planned business trip. He's had to cancel appointments and all of that, and he's holding you personally responsible."

"Sounds nice," Mason said.

"The way he tells it, it does, Perry— Can he do it?"

"What?"

"Hold you personally responsible."

"That depends," Mason said.

"On what?"

"On a variety of things— What I can't understand, Paul, is what's holding up the case against Gwynn Elston. They haven't any case."

"Now, wait a minute," Drake said, "that's the second barrel I was going to give you. This one's loaded pretty heavy."

"All right," Mason said. "What is it?"

"They have a report from ballistics," Drake said. "Frankline Gillett was killed by a shot from the gun that was thrown into the shrubbery. The fatal bullet came from that gun, there's no question about it."

"That still doesn't connect anything up with Gwynn Elston," Mason said.

"Yes, it does. Your client talked."

"What did she say?"

"Sobbed out the whole story."

Mason's eyes narrowed. "About the man with the broken-down car, the badge he showed her, the gun?"

"That's right."

"I was hoping she'd sit tight," Mason said, his voice showing his disappointment.

"They pulled the usual stunt," Drake said. "She got pretty fed up with jail, and they told her that the only reason she was being held was because she wouldn't talk, that if she'd tell the truth about what had happened and they could investigate her story and find out it was true, they'd let her go."

"So she told her story, and they said they couldn't go for it, is that it?"

"That's the funny part of it, Perry. They aren't issuing any press releases about her story, but they have made moulages of the tire tracks and footprints where the body was found. They find the treads match the tires on the car driven by Gwynn Elston. They find her footprints around the corpse. They find no other tire marks that can be identified, no other footprints."

Mason said, "All right, Paul. We've got to find the man who gave her the gun."

"They've already done that," Drake said.

"They've found the officer, Paul?"

"Officer, hell! It was Frankline Gillett who gave her that gun."

"How do they figure that, Paul?"

"Mrs. Gillett found the gun in her husband's suitcase about a week ago. She was worried. Gillett told her he'd found the gun in the street about four blocks from the house. He wanted to keep it. She didn't want him to have a gun around the kid."

"Can she identify it?"

"Yes. She wrote down the number, just in case. Then when Gillett said he was leaving on a trip and would be gone about a week, she told him to take the gun with him. She didn't want it left in the house. So he took the gun with him."

"Go on," Mason said.

"The day Gillett left his home coincided with the day Felting Grimes returned home from a business trip. He moved back into the Grimes household as Felting Grimes. He must have had the gun in his suitcase at the time. It was less than an hour from the time Gillett left that Grimes showed up at the house where your client was living."

Mason gave the information the benefit of long, thoughtful contemplation. "What does Nell Grimes say about the gun, Paul?"

"She never saw it," Drake said. "Not until Gwynn showed up with it and told the story about the officer who handed her the gun.

"Now, here's something else, Perry. The police aren't making the slightest effort to try to find any motorist who was stranded out there by Baxter's gates. They haven't called on any of the service stations to try to find if any of them sent out a service car. My men are the only ones who have been running down those leads.

"I can't understand it. Ordinarily they'd be trying to canvass all the garages and service stations just to prove Gwynn Elston's story was false and that there wasn't any car with a flat tire."

Mason frowned.

"That," Drake went on, "shows that they don't think enough of her story to waste time trying to disprove it."

Mason suddenly jumped to his feet.

"The hell it does!" he exclaimed. "It means they've found the guy! That's why they're not worried about him."

"If they've found him," Drake said, "and if his story substantiates hers, they'd turn her loose. No, Perry, you're barking up a wrong tree this time. They're going to tell her story and then show it's false by showing there wasn't any truth in her story."

"And how are they going to show that?" Mason asked.

"I don't know," Drake said. "I can't qualify as a mind reader, but there's something in the case that's going to crucify your client, Perry."

Mason said, "I tell you, Paul, they've *found* the fellow! Something in his story gives the prosecution ammunition—but I'll promise you one thing, if they ever produce a witness who will swear he rode in with Gwynn Elston, but swears he didn't give her any gun, I'll tear the guy apart. Now, they've found that fellow, Paul. I want *you* to find him. We have to know who he is."

Drake shook his head. "There wasn't anyone. The police are prepared to prove it. Remember, Perry, you have only the story of your client."

"And," Mason said, "they'll have only the story of this witness. If they want to slug it out in *that* corner, it'll be quite a session."

Drake said, "Don't forget that time element, Perry. The gates were closed and locked at ten. Gillet couldn't have got in after that time. His car must necessarily have been driven in through the gates.

"That leaves you a forty-five minute period for murder. It had to be committed within that time. It was during that time your client would have had to secure possession of the gun. It's during that time that she can't account for her movements and during that time she's invented this story of the mysterious officer who gave her the gun.

"She left the Gillett house at nine-fifteen. Mrs. Gillett is certain about the time. She ran into Gillett. He was probably waiting for her. He put it right up to her. She'd found out he was a bigamist and what was she going to do about it?

"If she'd tell the truth and say she had to kill him in self-defense, she's stand a chance. But remember, it was Gillett who had the gun. Remember, she called me shortly after nine-thirty and called you right afterwards.

"You can figure out what happened. Gillett stopped her. He wanted to talk. He had the gun. He wanted to go someplace where they wouldn't be disturbed, so they stopped near the Baxter estate. She reassured him in some way, may have let him make a little love to her—then she grabbed the gun, shot him, drove into the Baxter estate long enough to dump the body, and then fixed up this story about the officer."

Mason was thoughtful. "She'd have thought up a more convincing lie than that, Paul. She'd never have produced the gun. She'd have thrown it away in the first place."

"You can't say that," Drake told him, "until you know just what she was up against. Something happened and she was stuck with that gun. So she had to think up a story that would justify her having it in her possession."

Mason said, "Don't forget, Hamilton Burger, the district attorney, occasionally overlooks a point. He may not realize it, but he hasn't any way of proving that particular murder gun was in the defendant's possession. She had *a* Smith &

Wesson thirty-eight-caliber revolver. There are thousands of Smith & Wesson thirty-eight-caliber revolvers."

"And, of course," Drake said, "there's your action in tossing a cigarette case and a lighter over the fence."

"Sure," Mason said, "I was throwing out the first ball in the World Series, that's all. I wanted the police to get busy and search the premises, so I did something that would start them doing it. I just had an idea the murderer might have left the gun on the premises."

"And what gave you that idea?"

"Just good investigative technique," Mason said. "I wanted them to search the premises, and I'll bet you one thing, Paul. They've now combed every inch of that ground. That's one thing they'll have to give me credit for."

"Yes, I suppose they have," Drake said. And then added, "Now."

"That's all I wanted," Mason told him. "You be there in court tomorrow, Paul, and it may not be as one-sided as you and Hamilton Burger think it's going to be. And there's one other thing I want you to do."

"What's that?"

"Check the whereabouts of George Belding Baxter on the night of the murder."

"He was in Bakersfield," Drake said.

"He *says* he was in Bakersfield."

"He was," Drake said. "My men checked his story. He was in the motel there. After all, Perry we don't overlook the obvious."

"What do you mean, you checked his story?"

"Well," Drake said, "he registered in at six-thirty in the evening, said he was tired, was going to eat and go to bed. The motel has a restaurant connected with it. He ate there and signed the check—it's one of those high-class motels where you have hotel service. You sign checks, have a phone in your room and all that, and you check out in the morning."

Mason's eyes narrowed. "No one stood watch over him while he was in bed," he said. "What was to prevent him leaving the motel at seven o'clock, driving down and killing Frankline Gillett, then going back to the motel and checking out in the morning?"

Drake thought that over. "Nothing," he said.

Mason grinned.

After a moment, Drake said, "Got any proof that he did?"

"You got any proof that he didn't?" Mason asked.

# Chapter 14

Judge Harlan Laporte took the bench and announced, "This is the time previously fixed for the preliminary hearing in the case of the People of the State of California versus Miss Gwynn Elston."

"The People are ready," Farley Nelson, the trial deputy in the district attorney's office announced.

"Ready for the defendant," Mason said.

Judge Laporte looked down at Hamilton Burger, who was seated beside the deputy district attorney. "Do I understand the district attorney is also going to participate personally in the case?" he asked.

"The district attorney is personally going to participate in the case," Hamilton Burger said.

"Very well. Call your first witness."

Hamilton Burger arose and said, "If the Court pleases, there is one matter which I feel should take precedence; that is a motion on behalf of the attorneys representing George Belding Baxter to quash a subpoena which has been served upon him to appear as a witness for the defense."

"On what grounds?" Judge Laporte asked.

"Mr. Baxter's attorneys are here in court, but generally I will state that the grounds are that service of the subpoena constituted a misuse of the process of the court, that a deliberate attempt has been made to inconvenience Mr. Baxter, who is an exceedingly busy man; that the defendant hopes to obtain some advantage therefrom."

Judge Laporte looked down at Mason. "Is Mr. Baxter a necessary witness, Mr. Mason?"

"I consider him so, Your Honor. At least I feel there is a strong possibility he will be an important and necessary witness."

Hamilton Burger said, "If the Court please, this is a cut-and-dried case. The defendant will not put on any testimony at all, and we feel that if there is any reason for Mr. Baxter's presence here, counsel should now state to the Court what that reason is."

"I've stated," Mason said. "I want Mr. Baxter as a witness."

"A witness to what?"

"I'll disclose that at the proper time."

"If the Court please," Hamilton Burger said, "the prosecution at this time offers to stipulate any testimony defense counsel will state in good faith he expects Mr. Baxter to give."

Mason turned to the Court. "If the Court please," he said, "we submit that offer of stipulation is made simply for the purpose of embarrasing counsel; first, in getting the defense to disclose its case in advance; second, because Mr. George Belding Baxter has filed a suit against me, asking one hundred thousand dollars' damages for interfering with his business by abusing the process of the court and serving a subpoena on him."

"There is such a civil suit?" Judge Laporte asked Hamilton Burger.

"I believe there is, Your Honor."

"In that case," Judge Laporte said, "Mr. Baxter has elected his remedy. He can't eat his cake and have it, too. If he's going to sue Mr. Mason for damages, he can't ask to be excused as a witness on the strength of a stipulation. In view of the motion, I suggest that he elect which he wants to do, whether he wants to ask to quash the subpoena or whether he wants to proceed with his suit for damages."

Hamilton Burger turned to where George Belding Baxter was seated in the courtroom.

128

"I stand on my rights," Baxter said with cold savagery. "I also demand to be excused."

"Motion is denied," Judge Laporte snapped. "Proceed with your case, Mr. Burger."

Perry Mason walked over to where Paul Drake was seated just inside the bar and whispered, "That's the whole secret of the thing, Paul. Hamilton Burger is going to handle this very adroitly so that he'll help Baxter build up his damage suit against me. That's why he's here."

"The grapevine is, he's got a terrific surprise," Drake whispered back.

Mason grinned. "Well, we'll ride along and see what happens."

Farley Nelson called as his first witness a surveyor who introduced in evidence a map of the grounds of the Baxter estate and the house, all drawn according to scale.

Mason declined to cross-examine.

The next witness was Lt. Tragg, who testified to receiving a telephone call from Perry Mason advising him that there was a body at the Baxter estate; the witness had instructed radio officers to go to the place and preserve all evidence; the witness himself had made all possible speed to Perry Mason's office, hoping to catch the person who had been Perry Mason's source of information; Tragg stated that they had arrived too late; that they had, however, taken steps to intercept all taxis which had picked up passengers from stands near Mason's office building; that, in addition, they had instructed parking lots near the building to delay getting cars for all persons who had parked within an hour; that, as a result of these instructions, they had picked up the defendant, Gwynn Elston; that subsequently they had taken her to Mr. Mason's office; that he had advised her to say nothing; that she had in her purse a checkbook showing the stub of a check payable to Mason for five dollars; that subsequently they had arranged with the bank to photostat the check when it cleared, and that he had a photostat of that check, which had been duly endorsed by Perry Mason and cashed.

Lt. Tragg then went on to state that, after questioning Miss Elston briefly, he had gone to the Baxter estate and had personally investigated the case. He described the position of the body, what he had found; thereafter, upon being advised by the watchman at the gate that Perry Mason had appeared and had done certain things, Tragg had instituted a search of the premises and had uncovered a gun. The gun was offered for identification, a Smith & Wesson .38-caliber revolver which bore Tragg's mark etched on the handle.

"Cross-examine," Nelson said.

Mason said, "What were the certain things that I did?"

"I only know them by hearsay," Tragg said.

"Let's not be technical," Mason said. "Let's get on with the case. What were the things I did?"

"According to the officer at the gate," Tragg said, "you appeared at the gates and when you found the officer wouldn't let you inside, you opened a silver cigarette case, took out a cigarette, then tossed the cigarette case over the fence to within a very few feet of the place where the gun was found. Thereafter, you tossed a cigarette lighter in the same general direction."

"You recovered those?" Mason asked.

"I did."

"You placed your initials on them?"

"I scratched my initials on them, yes."

"You have those objects with you?"

"I do."

"Produce them, please."

Tragg produced them.

"I ask that they be marked for identification," Farley Nelson said.

"No objection," Mason said. "Introduce them in evidence, if you want to."

"We'll introduce them at the proper time," Nelson said. "Right now we only want these articles marked for identification."

"So ordered," Judge Laporte said.

"No further questions," Mason said.

Nelson called a photographer who had taken photographs of the body. This witness was followed by the autopsy surgeon, who had recovered the fatal bullet from the body of the deceased, and who fixed the time of death as between nine o'clock and midnight.

Mason declined to cross-examine either witness.

Nelson said, "Your Honor, it now becomes necessary to introduce evidence showing the identity of the corpse. This is rather painful and embarrassing, but since it is necessary, I am going to call Mrs. Frankline Gillett to the stand."

Mrs. Gillett, attired in black, took the oath and testified to her name, the fact that she had married Frankline Gillett eight years earlier, that she had been called on to identify the body at the morgue, and that the body was that of the man she had married.

"Cross-examine," Nelson said.

Mason said, "I'm sorry, Mrs. Gillett. I will try to make this as brief and as painless as possible. You state that you married your husband approximately eight years ago?"

"Yes."

"At that time, what was his occupation?"

"He was a salesman."

"Do you know the amount of his income?"

"It was not high. He worked on a guarantee and commissions."

"And worked hard?"

"Very hard."

"How long did he continue to work for this same company?"

"For about three years."

"Then what?"

131

"Then he was out of work for a while, then he got another job as a salesman. This was not quite as good as the first. He held it for about a year, then resigned and got another position which gave us more money."

"And then?" Mason asked.

"About two and a half years ago he announced that he was going in business for himself."

"And after that, what about your financial affairs?"

"After that, our financial affairs were very much better. He apparently made good money."

"Do you know anything at all about the nature of his business?"

"No."

"Since his death, have you been able to discover the nature of his business?"

"I have learned nothing about it," she said. "My husband was very close-mouthed about business affairs. He didn't want to discuss them with me. He told me that he was the provider for the family and that I was the homemaker. Since his death I have been unable to find any books of account, I have been unable to find anything that would indicate the source of his income. There is a joint checking account in which there was a balance of approximately three thousand dollars at the time of his death. I have since been given to understand that all deposits in this account were in the form of cash."

"Any other assets in the estate?" Mason asked.

"Certainly. We were buying a home on Tribly Way. We have that about two-thirds paid for. There is also a family car, which I drive for the most part, and another car which my husband drove."

"Did you," Mason asked, "find a gun in your husband's suitcase?"

"Objected to as not proper cross-examination," Nelson said.

"Overruled," Judge Laporte snapped. "She was asked

132

about what property her husband left. The Court frowns upon calling on a witness to give only a part of pertinent information. Answer the question."

Mrs. Gillett said slowly, "Shortly after my husband returned from his last business trip, I discovered a revolver in his suitcase. It was a thirty-eight-caliber Smith & Wesson revolver. I wrote down the number on it. That number was C232721.

"I asked my husband about it. . . . Do you want me to tell you what he said?"

"Go right ahead," Mason invited.

"He said he had found the gun lying near the side of the road about three blocks from the house. He said he had picked it up and had at first intended to report it to the police but had changed his mind because he felt they might, as he put it, pester him with questions.

"I didn't want to have a gun around the house and told him so. He promised he would keep it in the suitcase and away from our son. When he left the house on his last trip, he took that gun with him."

"Thank you," Mason said. "That's all."

"Now, Your Honor," Farley Nelson said, "this, of course, is one of the aspects of the case which has made it spectacular and has resulted in a great deal of newspaper notoriety. I think, however, in order to explain the circumstances in the case it will be necessary to call, rather reluctantly, Nell Arlington."

Nell Arlington came forward and was sworn.

"Where do you live?" Nelson asked.

"367 Mandala Drive."

"Did you go under the name of Nell Arlington while you were living there?"

"No, sir."

"Under what name?"

"That of Mrs. Felting Grimes."

"You considered Mr. Felting Grimes your husband?"

133

"Yes."

"You went through a marriage ceremony with him in Las Vegas, Nevada?"

"Yes."

"That was generally some eighteen months ago?"

"Eighteen months and ten days."

"You have seen the body that was identified as Frankline Gillett?"

"Yes."

"Was that the body of the man you married, the one whom you knew as Felting Grimes?"

"Yes."

"Are you familiar with the defendant in this case?"

"Yes. She had been my closest friend for some years."

"Where was she living on the tenth of this month?"

"With us, at 367 Mandala Drive."

"That was on the tenth of this month?"

"Yes."

"Will you please relate the events of that evening as nearly as you can remember them, Miss Arlington?"

The witness recounted Gwynn's story about the officer who had insisted on a ride and had given her his gun.

"Did you," Nelson asked, "see the body of the murdered man?"

"Yes."

"On the morning of the eleventh, do you remember when the defendant arose and came into the kitchen for breakfast?"

"Very well."

"Did you at that time know where the man you knew as Felting Grimes was?"

"No."

"When had you last seen him?"

"The day before, when he left on one of his trips."

Nelson said, "Are you familiar with the manner in which the defendant carried on her business transactions?"

"What do you mean by that?"

"The names of the prospects that she called on?"

"Oh, yes. I helped her a good deal in those matters. I acted both as a friend and as a secretary."

"Can you explain what you mean by acting as a secretary?"

"She would get lists, sometimes phone in, sometimes mailed in, of the prospects on whom she was to call. I would take down those lists when they came over the telephone in her absence, or see that she got the names of the prospects when they came by mail."

"Do you know how the name of Mrs. Frankline Gillett was received by the defendant?"

"Yes, it was received by mail. After she . . . well, after she was arrested, I found in the living room the list of prospects which contained that name— Here it is. The name, Mrs. Frankline Gillett, 671 Tribly Way, is the one here at the bottom. There are eleven names on the list."

"Was that list where the man you knew as your husband, Felting Grimes, could see it?"

"It was in the living room when I found it. Presumably it had been left there by the defendant."

"We ask that this be introduced in evidence," Nelson said.

"No objection," Mason said.

"Now," Nelson said, "I am going to ask you if, on the morning of Wednesday, the eleventh of this month, Mr. Mason called on you."

"He did."

"Who was with him?"

"His secretary, Miss Street."

"And what, if anything, did Mr. Mason try to get you to do at that time?"

"Objected to as incompetent, irrelevant and immaterial," Mason said. "It makes no difference what counsel for the defense may have tried to get the witness to do. Moreover, the question calls for a conclusion of the witness."

"If the Court please," Nelson said, "Mr. Mason was the attorney representing the defendant."

"Of course I was representing the defendant," Mason said. "I was also acting on my own. The defendant doesn't tell me how to try a case. I do what I think is best. If the prosecution wants to show that the defendant is bound by something that I did, let the prosecution show that the defendant knew about it and participated in it."

"I think that is correct," Judge Laporte said. "I'll sustain the objection."

"You may cross-examine," Nelson said.

"No questions," Mason said casually.

"No cross-examination?" Nelson asked in surprise.

"None whatever," Mason said.

Nelson conferred briefly with Hamilton Burger, then said, "I will call Peterson L. Marshall to the stand."

Marshall gave his name and address, stated that he was the proprietor of a sporting goods store, that he was well acquainted with George Belding Baxter, that Baxter had been a customer of his for some time and had a charge account there.

"I am going to show you a Smith & Wesson revolver, number C232721, and ask you if you recognize that revolver."

"I would like to check the number personally to make certain."

"Then check the number, please."

The witness checked the number, said, "Yes, I am familiar with that gun."

"Who sold that gun?"

"I did."

'You sold it personally?"

"Yes."

"To whom did you sell it?"

"To George Belding Baxter."

"Personally?"

"Yes, sir. Mr. Baxter came into the store and said he wanted a weapon for protection. He wanted something that was dependable and something that was not too bulky. I called his attention to this Smith & Wesson revolver with the two-inch barrel and the alloy metals which made it a very light, very convenient weapon. Mr. Baxter said he would take it."

"And what did you do?"

"Well," the witness said, hesitating, "we're not supposed to deliver guns the same day that they're purchased. We're supposed to hold them, but . . . well, under the circumstances, I simply dated the application back three days and delivered the gun to Mr. Baxter."

"You delivered it to Mr. Baxter personally?"

"Yes, sir."

"And that is this same weapon?"

"Yes, sir."

"You may cross-examine," Nelson said.

"No questions," Mason said.

"I will call Mrs. Minnie Crowder," Nelson said.

Mrs. Crowder identified herself as the housekeeper for George Belding Baxter.

Nelson said, "Now, on the evening of the tenth of this month, please tell us what you did."

"I finished up my work at about nine o'clock. The eleventh was my day off. I had been told that I didn't need to stay all night on the tenth, so I left the house just prior to nine in the evening—just a few minutes before. I had planned to return early on the morning of the twelfth. However, the police located me and interfered with my plans."

"What time did the police locate you?"

"Around two o'clock in the afternoon of the eleventh."

"I am going to show you this gun that has been marked for identification and ask you if you are familiar with it."

The witness took the gun, looked it over and and said, "Yes, I am."

"Did you ever have that gun in your possession?"

"I did."

"Who gave it to you, if anyone?"

"Mr. George Belding Baxter."

"And what happened to the gun?"

"I kept it in my bedroom and I took it with me when I walked at night. It fell from my coat pocket when I was walking on the night of the third. After I missed it, I returned to look for it but couldn't find it. So I said nothing to anyone."

"Why did Mr. Baxter give it to you?"

"Objected to as calling for a conclusion of the witness," Mason said, "also as being incompetent, irrelevant and immaterial."

"Sustained," Judge Laporte said.

Nelson said, "After the third of this month, or approximately the third of this month, you didn't see this gun again until when?"

"Until it was shown me by the police."

Mason said, "I dislike to interrupt counsel, but I think I am entitled to examine the witness on *voir dire.*"

"Go right ahead," Nelson invited. "However, I am just about finished with the witness and perhaps you would prefer to do this on cross-examination."

"It makes no difference to me," Mason said.

"Well, I'll ask just one more question. You saw this gun again on the eleventh of the month?"

"Yes."

"Where did you see it?"

"It was in the possession of Lieutenant Tragg. He showed it to me."

"Cross-examine," Nelson said.

"How do you know it's the same gun that Mr. Baxter gave you?" Mason asked.

"Well . . . well, I can tell it's the same gun. Mr. Gillett found it where I had dropped it."

"Do you know where you dropped it, the exact spot?"

"Not the exact spot. I dropped it while I was walking. That's where Mr. Gillett found it."

"You know *when* you dropped it?"

"Yes. It was the night of the third at about nine-thirty. I was taking a walk. I had the gun in my overcoat pocket. I slipped the coat off after I got hot walking, and when I got back, the gun was missing."

"Now, think carefully," Mason said. "Did you at any time while on that walk approach the hedge near where this gun was found by the police?"

"No."

"Not anywhere near the hedge?"

"I walked past it, but I didn't leave the surfaced road."

"But you could have lost the gun near the hedge?"

"I don't think so. I must have lost it when I slipped my coat off and folded it. I remember that was a hundred yards or so after I had left the gates and while I was walking along the pavement."

"Did you at any time make any note of the number of the gun given you by Mr. Baxter?"

"Of course not."

"That was a new gun?"

"He delivered it to me that day he purchased it."

"There were no distinguishing marks on the gun then, no scratches, no blemishes?"

"Certainly not. It was a brand-new gun."

"Are there any scratches or blemishes on the gun now?"

"I notice there are scratches on the handle. I believe those are marks made by Lieutenant Tragg."

"When did you first notice these marks?"

"After Lieutenant Tragg pointed them out to me."

"You have no independent recollection of any distinguishing marks being on the gun that was given you by Mr. Baxter?"

"Well . . . no."

"You don't know whether this is the gun given you by Mr. Baxter or whether it is simply one of the thousands of guns manufactured by the Smith & Wesson Company and sold throughout the nation, do you?"

"Well, if you want to put it that way, all I can say is that it looks like the gun Mr. Baxter gave me."

"Thank you," Mason said. "I want to put it that way. That's all."

Nelson called Alexander Redfield as a firearms and ballistics expert, and asked Redfield if he had examined the fatal bullet and if he had made tests to determine whether the fatal bullet had been fired from that weapon.

Redfield testified that he had made such tests.

"What can you state with reference to the fatal bullet having been fired from this particular weapon?"

"The fatal bullet was fired from this particular gun which I am holding in my hand, this Smith & Wesson revolver, number C232721," Redfield said.

"Now, if the Court please," Nelson said, "I move to introduce this weapon in evidence."

"Objected to as incompetent, irrelevant and immaterial, no proper foundation is laid," Mason said.

"What is your point?" Judge Laporte said.

"Simply this, Your Honor. There's one connecting link which is missing. George Belding Baxter took possession of this gun on the day it was purchased. Let *him* show that he gave the gun he purchased to the housekeeper."

"If the Court please, that doesn't make the slightest difference," Hamilton Burger said. "This weapon was found on the grounds where it had evidently been thrown. A gun, in every way similar in appearance to this weapon, was given to the housekeeper and then was missing from the housekeeper's possession. That's all we need. Actually, we don't need to show anything except that the gun was found on the grounds and that it is the murder weapon. That is all we need in order to get the weapon introduced in evidence. Anything else is simply for the purpose of showing the background and history of the weapon."

"The Court is included to agree with the district attorney," Judge Laporte said, "but why not simply call Mr. Baxter and have him testify that the gun he purchased was the gun he gave the housekeeper? Then you have connected up this weapon with its particular serial number."

"Because it isn't necessary," Hamilton Burger said.

Mason said dryly, "Because George Belding Baxter is suing me for a hundred thousand dollars' damages for serving a subpoena on him to testify of behalf of the defendant. *If* he should be called as a witness for the prosecution, it would then appear that his presence here had been necessary, and I wouldn't have damaged him by asking him to remain over to testify for the defense. That's the sole reason Hamilton Burger is here in court, to try and guide this case through the court so that it doesn't require the presence of George Belding Baxter as a witness."

Judge Laporte smiled faintly, then frowned thoughtfully. "Of course," he said, "the ordinary procedure would be to connect this weapon up, but . . . under the circumstances, I am inclined to agree with the district attorney that all that is really necessary in order to introduce the weapon in evidence is to show that it is the gun used in the murder and that the gun was found in a certain place.

"That lays the foundation for the introduction of the gun. Now then, if we are to go further than that and try to connect the gun up with the defendant, there is, of course, a certain element of hiatus there."

"We understand that, Your Honor. We'll cover that all

right," Hamilton Burger said confidently. "In fact, I think we have a witness who will cover that."

"Well," Judge Laporte said, "the Court is inclined to agree with you that a sufficient foundation has been laid to introduce the weapon in evidence. It will be received and marked an appropriate exhibit number."

Hamilton Burger couldn't restrain his expression of triumph. "Thank you, Your Honor."

Nelson called Corley L. Ketchum to the stand.

Ketchum, attired in a dark suit which had evidently seen years of service as a "best suit," seemed awkwardly ill at ease. He testified that he was the caretaker and gardener for the George Belding Baxter estate; that it was customary for the housekeeper to remain on duty until ten o'clock; that it was his duty to close and lock the gates at ten o'clock; that on the evening of the tenth he had not known that the housekeeper had left early in accordance with permission given by Mr. Baxter; and at two or three minutes before ten o'clock on that evening he had gone to the gates and had closed and locked them; that at that time he saw no car parked anywhere near the gates; that he had performed the simple, routine act of closing the gates and seeing that they were securely locked; that he had then returned to his caretaker's cabin and gone to bed. That prior to ten o'clock he had heard no car drive into the grounds but that on the other hand a car could have driven in without his hearing it.

"Cross-examination?" Nelson asked.

Mason shook his head.

An expert on moulage testified that he had acted under instructions of Lt. Tragg in making casts of tire treads on the car of the defendant as well as casts of the impressions left where the body was found; that he had matched those impressions; that he had also made impressions of foot tracks found near the body. Those impressions were introduced in evidence along with the impressions of the tires.

Again there was no cross-examination.

"I notice that it is approaching the hour of the noon adjournment," Judge Laporte said. "Do you have many more witnesses, Mr. Prosecutor?"

"I think one or two more will be all," Hamilton Burger said.

"Very well. Court will adjourn until two o'clock in the afternoon. The defendant is remanded to custody."

Judge Laporte left the bench. Paul Drake came pushing forward, said to Mason, "They've got a mystery witness, Perry. They're keeping him in the witness room. He's heavily guarded and no one can get in to see him."

"Man or woman?"

"Man."

"You're sure?"

"I got just a brief glimpse of his head, neck and shoulders as they hurried him in there. They've got a cordon of officers around the place. You'd think he was some visiting nabob the way they're acting."

"Can you describe him, Paul?"

"Well, he's about . . . oh, medium height, rather stocky build. I noticed he had quite a mop of dark, wavy hair."

"Wait a minute," Mason said, "wait a minute."

"What is it?" Della Street asked apprehensively.

"That," Mason said, "is the man who gave Gwynn Elston the gun. I told you they'd found him, Paul. That's the reason they weren't covering the service stations trying to trace the person who might have been called to go out and change a tire on that disabled car."

"There wasn't any disabled car, Perry," Drake said doggedly. "There couldn't have been. The time element is against you on that. I've checked it too carefully. There wasn't any time to send a repair car out and fix a flat tire."

Mason frowned. "Then there's some element in the case we don't know about, Paul."

"I tell you," Drake said, "they've got some big surprise. They're getting ready to lower the boom. There's something here that's going to blow your case clean out of the water."

"Well," Mason said, "we'll eat a light lunch and go into court and sit very lightly on our chairs. There may be an element here we don't know anything about, but once we get our hands on it we *may* surprise Burger."

Drake shook his head. "Not on this one, Perry. You can bet your bottom dollar they've checked and double-checked. There's an atmosphere of triumphant jubilation they simply can't conceal."

"We'll take things as they come," Mason said.

# Chapter 15

Immediately after court convened for the afternoon session, Hamilton Burger rose to his feet with the triumphant air of a magician pulling a rabbit out of the hat.

"I wish to call Carl Freeman Jasper to the stand," he said.

An officer stepped to the door of the witness room and held it open.

Mason, keeping a poker face, whispered to Gwynn Elston, "Be careful now. This is going to be a shock."

The door opened, and an individual in his late twenties walked rapidly into the courtroom.

Gwynn Elston's fingers dug into Mason's arm. She started to get to her feet, but Mason pushed her back down in the chair.

"It's him! It's him!" she said.

"Shut up," Mason whispered.

"He's the man who gave me the gun," she whispered.

Hamilton Burger, not unaware of the commotion and enjoying it immensely, said, "Step right up to the witness stand, Mr. Jasper. Take the oath, give your name and address to the court reporter, and be seated."

Hamilton Burger strode importantly up to the witness stand. "Mr. Jasper," he said, "what is your occupation?"

"I am a duly licensed private investigator."

"And you were such on the ninth of this month and on the tenth?"

"Yes, sir."

"Did you have any employment on that date?"

"I did, yes, sir."

"And who employed you?"

"A man who gave me the name of Felting Grimes."

"And the address that he gave you?"

"367 Mandala Drive."

"And did he give you a telephone number there?"

"He did."

Hamilton Burger turned to Mason with something of a bow. "If Court and counsel please," he said, "I would like to interrogate this witness so that I can make a consecutive sequence of events. In that way, there will be less confusion. Strictly speaking, it might be necessary for me to show his connection with the murder gun and with the defendant and then go back, but I trust Court and counsel will appreciate the advisability of having the narrative follow a certain sequence."

"By all means," Mason said, matching Hamilton Burger's suave courtesy. "We would like to have the issues clarified just as much as counsel for the prosecution. Go right ahead, Mr. District Attorney."

Hamilton Burger, who had evidently expected some objection and hoped to have an opportunity to argue that objection, said "Thank you," in the manner of a man whose first bomb has turned out to be a dud, and turned to the witness.

"You were employed by Mr. Grimes?"

"Yes, sir."

"When did that employment start?"

"On the morning of the tenth."

"And what did Mr. Grimes tell you to do?"

"If the Court please," Mason said, "I am willing to give the prosecutor a certain amount of leeway in order to get the preliminary matters disposed of, but I certainly see no reason for permitting a lot of hearsay evidence."

"It is part of the *res gestae*," Hamilton Burger said.

Judge Laporte shook his head. "Not unless it is first

shown to be part of the *res gestae* by better evidence than this, Mr. Prosecutor. The objection is sustained."

"Very well," Hamilton Burger said. "What did you *do?*"

"After receiving instructions from Mr. Grimes, I went to a house at 671 Tribly Way near Vista del Mesa, a house which was occupied by a Mr. and Mrs. Frankline Gillett."

"Did you know at that time that Frankline Gillett and Felting Grimes were one and the same person?"

"No, sir."

"When did you find out?"

"After I was called upon to identify the corpse which had been found at the estate of George Belding Baxter."

"And when was that?"

"That was on the evening of the eleventh and was after the body had been removed to the morgue."

"Now, then, as a result of your employment, what did you do?"

"I went to the Gillett residence, concealed my car in a place where it would not be conspicuous and kept the residence under surveillance."

"What were you looking for, if anything?"

"I was looking for the license number of any cars which drove up to the residence and stopped, and I was to get a description of any woman who entered the house."

"Were you given any particular description, any particular person to look for, any particular license number to watch for?"

"No, sir. I was just keeping the place under surveillance so I could describe the people, particularly women, who went in, and get the license numbers of the automobiles that were parked in front of the place, or that turned in at the driveway."

"And then what were you to do?"

"As soon as I had any license number of any car, or as

soon as there had been any developments, I was to telephone my office, and they would report to Grimes."

"When did you make your first telephone call to your office?"

"On the evening of the tenth."

"And what car did you report at that time?"

"I reported the car which I have since ascertained is owned by the defendant, Gwynn Elston. I reported the license number and gave a detailed description of Miss Elston; that is, as much of a detailed description as I could give."

"How long was that after Miss Elston had driven up to the house?"

"Within about three minutes."

"And you made this report by telephone?"

"Yes, sir."

"Where did you make the report? That is, where did you find the telephone?"

"I had a communications system in my automobile and I was able to relay a message to my office so that the message could, in turn, be relayed to Felting Grimes."

"And how could Felting Grimes reply to you?"

"Only by giving instructions to the person in my office, who in turn could relay them to me in my car over the short-wave communicating system."

"Now then, what happened after that?"

"I remained on the job."

"And then what happened?"

"While Miss Elston was still at the house and within approximately twenty minutes after I had finished placing the call over my short-wave communications system, Mr. Felting Grimes drove up; that is, the man whom I had come to know as Felting Grimes drove up. I now know, of course, that his real name was Frankline Gillett and that the name Felting Grimes was another name he was using in connection with his other house, or perhaps I should say his other identity."

"Now then," Hamilton Burger said, "I think this definitely is a part of the *res gestae*. What did your client instruct you to do at that time?"

Judge Laporte looked down at Perry Mason. "Any objections?"

"I think not," Mason said. "If the Court please, I think we should go into this. It is becoming exceedingly interesting."

"I thought you would find it *quite* interesting," Hamilton Burger said.

The witness said, "Mr. Grimes, as I knew him at that time and as I shall refer to him in my testimony, instructed me to leave my post and to follow him."

"Now, your post was there on Tribly Way?"

"Yes, sir."

"How far is that from the estate of George Belding Baxter?"

"Well, that depends on whether you mean—"

"I mean the entrance to the estate of George Belding Baxter, the iron gates."

"Around a quarter of a mile."

"And it is along that road that the defendant drove in going and coming?"

"It is along that road she would drive. I didn't follow her."

"But that is the road she would necessarily follow?"

"Yes."

"And the Baxter estate; that is, the gates to the Baxter estate, are within easy walking distance of the house on Tribly Way?"

"It depends on what you mean by easy," the witness said.

"The Court will take judicial cognizance that a quarter of a mile is a quarter of a mile," Judge Laporte said. "It is four hundred and forty yards, a distance which can be covered very easily in a period of approximately five to seven minutes by a pedestrian walking at a reasonable rate of speed. Let's get on with the case."

"Very well. What did you do?" Hamilton Burger asked.

"I followed the car driven by Felting Grimes to the George Belding Baxter estate."

"Then what?"

"I may state," the witness said, "that at this entrance to the George Belding Baxter estate the road widens as it is joined by the driveway from the Baxter estate, and that was the first place where we could conveniently park our cars off the road where we would not be in danger of being hit."

"Very well, go ahead," Hamilton Burger said. "What happened?"

"We stopped our cars. My client told me that it was absolutely necessary that I devise some excuse to stop the person whom I had seen go into the Gillett house when she started back toward the city. He said I simply must get in the car with her and remain with her until she reached a telephone booth and that I must learn the number she called. He said she was rather friendly and that I was to win her confidence. He said I was to spend the night with her, if possible."

"What did you do?"

"I protested the assignment would be difficult. My client brushed aside my protestations. He asked me if I had a gun. I said I did not. He thereupon handed me a revolver and said that if I had to do so, I was to shoot out a rear tire as the car went past. He said she wouldn't be able to tell what I had done, that the report of the gun would sound like a blowout."

"Did you agree to do this?"

"I let him give me the gun. I had mental reservations as to what I would do, but my client was so agitated I decided not to argue with him."

150

"What *did* you do?"

"I parked my car on the side of the road. I raised up the lid of the trunk. I tried to make it appear I was having tire trouble. I decided that if I could get a ride with this girl I would do so."

"What did your client do?"

"He said he would follow along behind us after I had secured a ride with the woman, who, by the way, I now know was Miss Elston, the defendant in this case."

Hamilton Burger said, "Your client gave you a gun?"

"Yes, sir."

"And you took it?"

"Reluctantly, yes, sir."

"And you planned to win the confidence of the defendant?"

"Yes, sir."

"And get her to confide in you?"

"Yes, sir."

"You took this gun your client gave you?"

"Yes, sir."

"What kind of a gun was it?"

"A thirty-eight-caliber Smith & Wesson revolver with a two-inch barrel."

"I show you the gun which has been heretofore marked as People's Exhibit G and ask you if this is the gun."

"Now, just a moment," Mason said. "I submit that that question calls for a conclusion of the witness. I would like to be permitted to ask questions on *voir dire.*"

"You may ask your questions on *voir dire,*" Judge Laporte said.

"Did you take the number of the gun when Mr. Grimes handed it to you?" Mason asked.

"No, sir."

"Did you look the gun over carefully?"

"I looked it over carefully."

"Were there any distinguishing marks on that gun which

would enable you to swear that this gun, People's Exhibit G, is the same gun that he gave you?"

"I failed to find any distinguishing marks."

"Then," Mason said, "you can't swear that the gun, People's Exhibit G, was the gun that he gave you."

"Only by its general appearance."

"As a private detective you are familiar with firearms?"

"Generally, yes."

"You know that the Smith & Wesson Company makes and sells thousands of these guns of an identical model?"

"I assume so, yes."

"You have seen many of these revolvers on display?"

"Yes."

"Now," Mason said, "do you yourself carry a gun when you are acting as a private detective?"

"At times."

"On this evening of the tenth of this month, did you yourself carry a gun?"

"No, sir. That's why my client gave me this gun."

"And you cannot state positively that this gun, People's Exhitit G, was the gun that Felting Grimes gave you?"

'No, sir, I can't swear to it. All I can swear is that it was a gun identical in appearance."

"That concludes my *voir dire* examination," Perry Mason said.

"Very well. Go on, Mr. Prosecutor," Judge Laporte said, leaning forward with his elbows on the bench, peering down at the witness, his manner showing his extreme interest.

"But," Hamilton Burger said, "you can't detect anything in the appearance of the gun, People's Exhibit G, which was in any way *different* from the gun that the man you refer to as Felting Grimes handed you at that time?"

"No, sir."

"Very well. Then what happened?"

"My instructions were that I was to stop the person driving the car, that no matter what expedient I had to use I was to get in the car with her and drive with her for a ways until she made a phone call."

"And then what happened?"

"Mr. Grimes said that he would drive down the road and park where he could keep out of sight. Then he looked down the road and couldn't seem to find a place. I suggested that it might be possible for him to drive just inside of the George Belding Baxter estate, turn his car around and be in a position where he could emerge from the estate as soon as Miss Elston had driven by."

"And what did Mr. Grimes do?"

"He accepted my suggestion, drove into the Baxter estate and waited just inside the gates."

"And what happened after that?"

"Within a matter of minutes I saw headlights coming down the street. I stepped out into the highway and waved my arms and held the beam of my flashlight on the windshield."

"And then what happened?"

"The car was driven by the defendant. She came to a stop, but the windows were up and the doors were locked. She rolled down the right-hand window a matter of about three inches, but she wouldn't lower it any more, or unlock the car door."

"So what did you do?"

"I walked to the side of the car. She put the window down about an inch so she could hear my voice and asked me what I wanted. So I flashed a badge and told her I was an officer working on a very important case; that I had tire trouble, and my spare was flat so I couldn't put it on the wheel in that condition; that I didn't have a jack, that it was necessary for me to go to the nearest service station in order to get assistance, that I wished to ride with her."

"And what happened?"

"She hesitated, so I then told her that she had nothing to fear, that not only was I an officer, but that I would give her my gun, that she could hold it in her lap and that in the event I made any attempt to molest her in any way she could use the gun."

"And then what happened?"

"She fell for that approach. I had turned on all the charm I could and I think she rather liked it. She opened the door, I got in the car, put the gun on her lap."

"And what happened after that?"

"She seemed glad to have me for company. When she drove to this first little town, Vista del Mesa, I looked the service stations over. I saw one that had a phone booth and I asked her to stop there. I said I wanted to get the attendant to go back to fix my tire."

"And she stopped?"

"Yes, sir."

"What did you do?"

"I went to the attendant and asked him where the rest rooms were, then I circled the station and slipped up behind the phone booth before she even got out of the car."

"Then what did you do?"

"I crouched down at the back of the booth. I watched her dial a number I have since learned was that of the Drake Detective Agency, and ask for Perry Mason. I then watched her hang up and dial another number which I have since learned was that of the Hollywood Brown Derby. Again she asked for Perry Mason."

"Was there a conversation?"

"There was."

"Did you hear her words?"

"Very distinctly."

"What did you hear her say?"

"I heard her say Felting Grimes was a heel and that someone should kill him. She was silent while the party at the other end of the line said something, and then she said she really meant it, that if someone killed him it would be good riddance."

"Anything else?"

"She made an appointment over the phone with this person with whom she was talking for a ten-thirty appointment the next morning."

"Then what happened?"

"My client had been following us. He had parked his car on a side street. I saw that she was getting ready to hang up and leave the phone booth, so I backed away from it, sprinted over to my client's car, and I was there by the time she came out of the phone booth."

"You told him of the conversation?"

"All of it."

"What effect did that have on him?"

"It disturbed him greatly. He told me to get in his car. He drove me back to the Baxter estate where I'd left my car. He said the fat was in the fire."

"And then what happened?"

"My client told me that there was nothing further for me to do, that my assignment was finished for the evening, that he would call me the next day if he needed me any more. He asked me to return the gun, and I explained I'd left it in the car with Miss Elston, and that annoyed him. He berated me for that, and I told him it was his fault, that I'd have had the gun back and probably could have had a date with the subject if he hadn't ordered me to get in his car and driven me off."

"And what did he say?"

"He said the woman wasn't kidding in what she'd said over the phone, that she'd kill him, and that now she had a gun—"

"Move to strike this out as hearsay," Mason said.

"It shows the state of mind of the deceased," Hamilton Burger said.

The judge nodded. "I'm going to let it stay in. I thing it's all inseparably linked together anyway. It's *res gestae.*"

"And then what did you do?" Burger asked the witness.

"I closed the lid of the trunk on my car, turned on the ignition and the headlights, and drove off."

"And where was your client at that time?"

"He was standing out in the rain by his car."

"And where was his car?"

"By the gates of the George Belding Baxter estate."

"And were those gates open or closed?"

"At that time the gates were open."

"Do you know what time it was?"

"I do."

"What time was it?"

"Ten minutes before ten o'clock."

"How do you know the time?"

"I looked at my watch and made a note of it because I was signing off for the day."

"Now, when you left the defendant at the service station, you left her in possession of that gun which your client had given you?"

"Yes, sir."

"I will ask you one more question," Hamilton Burger said. "At the time your client gave you the gun, did you make any examination of it?"

"Yes, sir."

"What did you do? What was the examination?"

"I asked Mr. Grimes if the gun was loaded. He said it certainly was. However, as is my custom with firearms, I swung open the cylinder and looked at it."

"You mean you looked at the cylinder?"

"Yes."

"At the cartridges in the cylinder?"

"Yes."

"What can you say, with reference to the gun being loaded?"

"There were six fully loaded thirty-eight-caliber cartridges in the cylinder."

"Not one of the cartridges in the gun had been discharged at that time?"

"Not at that time, no."

"You're positive?"

"Yes."

Hamilton Burger turned to Perry Mason. "Go ahead and cross-examine," he said, and the way he made the statement, if was more of a challenge than an invitation.

Mason got to his feet, studied the witness thoughtfully for a moment.

"The gun, People's Exhibit G, is a rather popular make, is it not, particularly with peace officers and detectives?"

"It is. It is particularly popular with plain-clothes operators, chiefs of police and persons of that sort who need to have a weapon handy at all times but don't care about having one that is as heavy or as conspicuous as the weapon carried by a uniformed officer."

Mason walked over to the exhibit table, picked up the gun which was People's Exhibit G, walked over to the witness. "Now," he said, "is there any way by which you can identify this gun or differentiate it from any other gun of the same make, except for the fact that People's Exhibit G has a tag attached to the trigger guard identifying it as an exhibit in this case?"

The witness studied the gun as Mason held it out for his inspection.

"No," he said.

Mason returned Exhibit G to the clerk's desk, walked back to confront the witness. "You can't swear on your oath that this gun, People's Exhibit G, is the gun you gave to the defendant?"

"No, sir, I can't swear to it. All I can swear is that it is a gun that is similar in appearance."

"You were hired to worm your way into the confidence of the defendant?"

"To find out whom she called on the phone, and what her plans were."

"And you turned on all your charm when you talked with her?"

"I wanted to get her to take me into her confidence."

"So you could betray that confidence?"

"So I could report to my client."

"And you were prepared to make love to the defendant, to lie to her, or to do anything else that might be necessary to accomplish your purpose?"

"I had a job to do. In my line of work we can't always choose the means by which we can do a job."

"Answer the question, you were prepared to make love to the defendant?"

"Yes."

"To lie to her?"

"Yes."

"You feel that your job requires you to lie from time to time?"

"Yes."

"And you are willing to lie for money?"

"Not for money."

"What, then?"

"To get the information I have to get."

"And that's the way you make your living?"

"I have a profession."

"You make money from it?"

"A living, yes."

"Answer the question, you make money from it?"

"Yes."

"And lie in order to make that money?"

"Oh, all right, if you want to put it that way."

Mason said, "That's all."

"That concludes the People's case," Hamilton Burger said. "It now becomes very apparent what happened, Your

Honor. The decedent was alive and well at the time this witness left him at ten minutes to ten. Thereafter the defendent had possession of the murder weapon. We know that Gillett's death must have occurred before ten o'clock, because the gates of the George Belding Baxter estate were closed and locked at that time. We know that the defendant had the murder weapon in her possession the next morning. We know that she was at home at the house on Mandala Drive, where she lived, all night, because Nell Arlington, known to the defendant as Nell Grimes, the wife of Felting Grimes, would have known if the defendant had gone out during the night. The next morning, when she showed the gun to the witness, Nell Arlington, there was an empty shell under the hammer.

"This is, therefore, one of the most perfect cases of circumstantial evidence we have had in our office. The circumstances speak louder than words and more emphatically than any words or any denial. The defendant found out the decedent had been following her. She must have followed him back to the Baxter estate. The minute the witness Jasper drove away, this defendant followed Gillett into the grounds, murdered him, and drove out of the grounds—all before ten o'clock when the gates were closed and locked.

"Those gates were kept closed and locked all night. The murder took place on the night of the tenth. There was only one ten-minute period when it could have taken place, and the defendant had the murder weapon in her possession during that time.

"These facts can't be questioned or explained away. They are physical facts which shout the guilt of this defendant."

"Are you attempting to argue the case at this time?" Mason asked.

"Call it argument if you want to," Hamilton Burger said. "I was simply summing up the testimony for the benefit of the Court."

"Well, let's keep the procedure in an orderly pattern," Judge Laporte said. "You have rested your case, Mr. District Attorney. Does the defense have any evidence?

"After all, at this time the Court is only concerned in finding out whether a crime has actually been committed, and there's no question about that, and finding out whether there are reasonable grounds to connect the defendant with the crime. There seems to be no question that the evidence certainly does this."

Hamilton Burger, grinning triumphantly, sat down, leaving Mason to argue with the judge.

"If the Court please," Mason said, his manner showing he was thinking fast and trying to orient himself with the new developments in the case, "the Court has stated a correct rule of law. If the district attorney had never put this last witness on the stand, he would certainly have been entitled to an order binding the defendant over for trial, but the district attorney took one step too far. He has now introduced evidence which conclusively establishes the innocence of the defendant. He can't now ask to have the defendant bound over, despite the fact that up to this last point there was evidence tending to connect the defendant with the commission of the crime."

"Is it counsel's contention that the last witness conclusively proves the defendant innocent?" Burger demanded incredulously.

"It is," Mason said.

"Proceed with your argument," Burger said with exaggerated politeness. "I would like very, very much indeed to hear how counsel can justify such a preposterous position at this time."

"The answer is quite simple," Mason said. "It now appears that the last witness, Carl Freeman Jasper, had the murder weapon in his possession, that he was the last person to see the decedent alive, that while he has told a story which *endeavors* to explain away those facts, the situation remains that this witness had the murder weapon in his possession, was with the decedent a few minutes before the time of the decedent's death.

"Under the evidence, the finger of suspicion points more damningly to this last witness than it does to the defendant. He admits that the gun was in his possession. He admits that he was the last person to see the decedent alive. And the Court will notice particularly that all of the time that the district attorney was asking him questions about the gun, the district attorney *never once dared to ask him the simple question, quote, Did you kill the man you knew as Felting Grimes or did you have anything to do with his death, unquote.* The district attorney didn't dare to ask him that question."

Mason sat down.

Hamilton Burger, his face flaming, jumped to his feet. "Why, Your Honor," he shouted, "that's the most preposterous argument I have ever heard in my life! That is . . . why, that is sheer poppycock. At this time the prosecution asks leave to reopen the case, to put the witness once more on the stand and ask him that question which counsel has said we didn't dare to ask him. We'll show counsel what we dare to do!"

Mason smiled. "The defense has no objection, Your Honor. Let the prosecution reopen the case."

Hamilton Burger turned to face the courtroom. "Carl Jasper," he shouted, "resume the witness stand, please."

Jasper came forward.

"Did you kill Felting Grimes?"

"No."

"That's all," Hamilton Burger said. "You may leave the stand."

"Just a minute," Mason said, "I would like to cross-examine the witness. Mr. Jasper, when did Mr. Grimes first employ you?"

"Objected to," Hamilton Burger said, "as being already asked and answered."

Judge Laporte said, "I thing that's correct, Mr. Mason. I think the evidence shows that he was employed on the ninth."

"This question," Mason said, "is when Mr. Grimes *first* employed Mr. Jasper."

"And the question has been asked and answered," Hamilton Burger said, raising his voice.

"I think that's correct," Judge Laporte said.

Mason, who had been studying the witness' face, said, "Very well, I'll reframe the question. Had you been employed by Mr. Grimes prior to the ninth day of this month?"

"Objected to," Hamilton Burger said. "Incompetent, irrelevant and immaterial, not proper cross-examination and not proper recross-examination. My question on redirect examination was limited to the question of whether or not he had been guilty of a murder."

"And my question on recross-examination," Mason said, "is for the purpose of showing bias on the part of the witness or interest in the outcome of this case."

"I'm going to permit that last question," Judge Laporte said.

"If the Court please," Hamilton Burger said, "I don't like to continue to argue with the Court, but it would certainly seem that this is going far afield, that it is not proper cross-examination and, in particular, is not proper recross-examination at this time."

"I think counsel is entitled to go into it on a question of bias or interest," Judge Laporte said. "The Court confesses that it was wondering just how it happened that Mr. Grimes called this witness to act as a private detective, one might say, out of a clear sky.

"Answer the question, Mr. Witness."

162

Jasper said, "I was first employed by Mr. Grimes about two and one half or three years ago."

"What!" Hamilton Burger said, his voice and face showing his surprise.

"I haven't the exact date," Jasper said. "It was about two and one half or three years ago."

Mason said, "You were employed by Mr. Grimes in connection with some fingerprint evidence, were you not?"

"Yes, sir. He gave me some latent fingerprints and a set of ten fingerprints and asked me if I could determine whether the latent fingerprints were the same as any of the fingerprints shown in the set of printed fingerprints."

"Were they?"

"Yes, sir."

"Did you know whose fingerprints those were?"

"No, sir."

"There was no identification on the fingerprints?"

"No, sir."

"How were the printed fingerprints handed to you?"

"They were given to me by Mr. Grimes."

"I mean, where did they originally come from, do you know?"

"No, sir."

"They were printed fingerprints?"

"Yes."

"They had been printed on a piece of paper."

"What do you mean by that?"

"In other words, the fingerprints, if I understand you correctly, were the same type of fingerprint evidence that is put out by police officers in seeking to locate a criminal?"

"Yes, sir."

"These printed fingerprints had been cut from the circular so that all you had were the fingerprints?"

"Yes, sir."

"Did that arouse your curiosity?"

"Somewhat."

"And did you classify those fingerprints and take steps to find out the person whose fingerprints they were?"

"No, sir. Actually, I thought of it and considered doing so, but finally decided against it."

"Did you return those printed fingerprints to Mr. Grimes?"

"Yes."

"And from that moment on you knew, or had reason to believe, that Felting Grimes had located some person who was wanted by the police?"

"I . . . well . . . I guess so."

"But hadn't turned that person in to the police?"

"Well, yes."

"And you knew that was a perfect setup for blackmail?"

"I didn't think of it in that light."

"Let's not be naïve, Mr. Jasper. You knew what the decedent had in mind, didn't you?"

"I might have suspected it."

"And because you did suspect it, you were smart enough to classify those fingerprints and find out from the FBI records whose prints they were, weren't you?"

"I . . . well . . . yes."

"Then you lied when you said a moment ago that you didn't run down those prints?"

"Yes."

"And those prints were the prints of Collington Halsey, one of the men most wanted by the FBI, weren't they?"

"Yes."

"And thereafter you blackmailed Felting Grimes, just as Grimes was blackmailing Halsey, didn't you?"

"I did no such thing. I resent that charge. It is an untruth."

"How much money did you receive from Felting Grimes during the last two and one half years?"

"Nothing, except for services rendered."

"How much money?"

"Just what I was paid for various professional services."

"How much money? Remember, you're under oath."

"Only what my services were worth."

"How much money?"

"I can't recall."

"Five thousand dollars?"

"Possibly."

"Ten thousand?"

"Perhaps."

"Twenty thousand?"

"I can't recall."

"Thirty thousand?"

"No, not that much."

"That's all," Mason said. "As a blackmailer and a perjurer with the murder weapon in your possession, the Court can draw its own conclusions."

Judge Laporte looked down at Perry Mason thoughtfully. "Mr. Mason, would you mind telling the Court why you asked the witness the question about the fingerprints? Apparently there is something in this case which none of us knows about but which you must have deduced from the testimony of this witness and . . . well, the Court has an idea there may be something in this case that you have in mind which might be interesting to the Court."

"It was just a wild shot in the dark, Your Honor," the discomfited Hamilton Burger said. "Quite evidently that's all it was."

"If it was a shot in the dark," Judge Laporte said, "counsel seems to have an unerring aim."

"I think, if the Court please," Mason said, "if I could recall one witness for further cross-examination, we might clear the matter up."

"I object," Hamilton Burger said. "If counsel wants to call a witness, let him call the witness as a witness for the defense. The case had been closed, the prosecution has rested."

"The prosecution reopened the case to put Mr. Jasper back on the stand," Judge Laporte said thoughtfully, weighing the point. "A court is not merely a place where counsel can practice mental gymnastics but is a place where an attempt is made to ascertain the truth or falsity of charges that have been made and where justice can be done."

Mason said, "If the Court please, I would like to see the typewritten list of names, the prospects which were given to the defendant and which list included the name of Mrs. Frankline Gillett. I think perhaps then I can come nearer answering the Court's question."

Mason walked over to the clerk's desk, took the exhibit in his hand, returned with it and bent over Della Street's chair.

"Take a look at this, Della," he whispered. "Get Paul Drake to check with you. See if the typewriting on the last name on that list is the same as the typewriting on the other names. If it isn't, shake your head when I look at you. If it is, nod your head."

Perry Mason walked over to stand in front of the Court. "If the Court please," he said, "there are certain aspects of this case which I feel the Court should take into consideration. I feel that the Court should permit me to recross-examine one of the witnesses. However, if—"

"We object to reopening the case," Hamilton Burger said. "Counsel has had his opportunity. Let's face the facts. Under the circumstances of this case, the defendant is the *only* one who *can* be guilty of this murder."

"If the Court please," Mason said, "there are several distinct possibilities. In the first place, Carl Jasper *could* well be guilty of the murder. He could have killed the decedent *before* turning the gun over to the defendant."

Mason paused, stood for a moment looking at Della Street.

She looked up and shook her head.

Hamilton Burger said, "May it please the Court, what counsel is trying to do is only too apparent.

"As is usual in these preliminary hearings, counsel for the defense has no intention whatever of making any bona fide defense or of putting any witnesses on the stand.

"Counsel has, however, abused the process of the court in trying to blackmail Mr. George Belding Baxter by using the power of the court's subpoena to inconvenience Mr. Baxter to such an extent that certain concessions could be obtained by the defendant.

"Mr. Baxter is made of sturdier stuff. He refused to be blackmailed, he refused to be intimidated. He has filed a suit against Mr. Mason for one hundred thousand dollars.

"In the event Mr. Mason does not put Mr. Baxter on the stand, it will show that Mr. Baxter's complaint is well taken. If he is forced by the Court to do so, Mr. Mason will probably make an attempt to call Mr. Baxter, but what he now wants to do is to confuse the issues to such an extent that he can claim, with some attempt at justification, when the Baxter case comes up for trial, that he subpoenaed Mr. Baxter because he *thought* that under certain issues which might develop in the case, Mr. Baxter would be a necessary witness and that the service of the subpoena on Mr. Baxter was made in good faith.

"Now, that's all there is to this case. There isn't any question but that the evidence indicates the defendant's guilt. There isn't anybody else who *could* have been guilty. There is some evidence of blackmail. My office will look into that. But what counsel is now trying to do is to confuse the issues to such an extent that he can make the Court an unwitting accomplice in building a fabricated defense which he can use when the suit filed by Mr. Baxter comes to trial."

Judge Laporte frowned. "Of course," he said, "the Court takes certain matters into consideration in a situation of this sort. The court can well appreciate the logic of the prosecution's position and the temptation which doubtless exists for the defense counsel to raise a series of questions which would make it appear that under certain circumstances he might have been justified in calling Mr. Baxter to the stand."

Mason said, "May it please the Court, I intend to call Mr. Baxter to the stand."

"You intend to put on a defense?" Judge Laporte asked.

"I do," Mason said.

"Very well," Judge Laporte said. "I'm going to make rather an unusual ruling. I'm going to let the defendant go ahead and put on a case. If, during the course of that case, it appears that there is some actual reason for his motion to recall one of the prosecution's witnesses for further cross-examination, I am going to suspend proceedings on the defendant's case and grant the motion so that the defendant can recall the prosecution's witness."

"Just let him put George Belding Baxter on the stand," Hamilton Burger said. "Let him try it. I defy him."

"There is no occasion for any such outburst on the part of the prosecutor," Judge Laporte said. "Put on your case, Mr. Mason."

"As the first witness for the defense," Mason said, "I call George Belding Baxter to the stand."

"Come forward and be sworn, Mr. Baxter," Judge Laporte said.

Baxter glanced meaningly at Hamilton Burger as he walked forward and held up his hand and took the oath as a witness.

As Baxter sat down, Hamilton Burger stood up.

"If it please the Court," he said, "I am going to object to any questions asked of this witness which are not absolutely and directly pertinent to this case. I am not going to permit counsel to go on a fishing expedition without having the record show that is exactly what it is."

"Under the circumstances," Judge Laporte said, "I feel that the Court will endeavor to protect the witness against what may be called a fishing expedition."

"And, if the Court please," Mason said, "by the same token, since this is a hostile witness, I feel that I should be entitled to ask leading questions."

"The Court is inclined to agree with you on that, Mr. Mason. Proceed."

George Baxter sat in the witness chair, glowering at Perry Mason, prepared to attack the lawyer at the first opportunity.

"How long have you held the property known as the Baxter estate?" Mason asked.

"Objected to as incompetent, irrelevant and immaterial," Hamilton Burger said.

"Overruled," Judge Laporte said.

"I have held it for some seventeen years, Mr. Mason," George Baxter said, "and I want to state that not only do I consider this has nothing to do with the issues involved in this case, but I know nothing whatever about the facts in this case. I was in Bakersfield, California, on the night of the tenth. I knew nothing whatever about the murder until the eleventh, when I returned to my office here in the city."

Baxter smiled triumphantly and sat back in the witness chair.

Mason said, "I will then ask you, Mr. Baxter, how long you have known that your man, Corley L. Ketchum, was actually Collington Halsey, wanted by the police in connection with a holdup and murder."

Hamilton Burger jumped to his feet to make an objection, then paused as he saw Baxter's face.

The triumphant smile had fled from Baxter's countenance. He seemed almost to wilt inside his clothes.

Hamilton Burger delayed for a fateful moment before saying, "Objected to, if the Court please. Incompetent, irrelevant and immaterial."

Hamilton Burger's hesitancy had made a sufficient impression on Judge Laporte so that the judge had also turned to glance at the witness, and the ruling came with unexpected promptitude. "The objection is overruled. Answer the question."

Baxter sat silent on the witness stand.

"Do you understand the question?" Mason asked.

"I understand it."

"Are you going to answer it?"

Baxter took a long, deep breath, said, "I have known it for some years."

"What relation is Mr. Ketchum to you?"

"He is my brother."

"And you gave him asylum knowing that he was wanted by the police?"

"Yes."

"And some two and a half years ago the decedent, Frankline Gillett, uncovered your secret?"

"He discovered the identity of my brother, yes."

"And demanded blackmail?"

"Yes."

Hamilton Burger said, "Oh, if the Court please, this is getting so far afield that—"

"If you're about to make an objection, the objection is overruled," Judge Laporte said. "I think we're now beginning to get to the nub of the case. I take it, Mr. Mason, you have deduced this from the fact that the fingerprints which were submitted to the detective, Carl Freeman Jasper, were actually those of Collington Halsey?"

"Yes, Your Honor."

The witness said, "Your Honor, I may as well make a clean breast of the entire situation. My brother, who has been masquerading under the name of Corley L. Ketchum, was actually Collington Halsey, and my real name is George Belding Halsey. My brother had at one time been engaged in a life of crime with Gorman Gillett, who was the father of Frankline Gillett.

"Gorman Gillett served time and was released. I will never know how it happened that Gorman Gillett uncovered my identity, but I think it was because of an article which appeared in the *Saturday Evening Post*. We tried to keep my brother in the background in that article, but without our knowing it the photographer snapped a picture of my brother and myself looking over some plans, and the caption of the picture was: 'George Belding Baxter and his gardener, Corley L. Ketchum, study plans for architectural landscaping.'

"It was shortly after that Frankline Gillett called on my brother and made demands. We have been paying blackmail ever since."

Hamilton Burger started to get up and say something, then abruptly dropped back into his chair.

"Now, tell us what happened on the night of the tenth," Mason said.

"There was nothing that we could do," the witness went on. "We were powerless. We had to submit to the blackmail. My brother's fingerprints were on file and he was wanted by the FBI. By having him living with me and posing as a humble and rather low-salaried gardener and caretaker, we were able to keep his identity a secret. However, after his identity was uncovered by Gorman Gillett and that information reached his son, Frankline, we had to pay, and we had to pay through the nose. However, I sometimes doubt that Gorman ever knew what his son was doing, or how much he was exacting.

"When I was in Bakersfield on the tenth, I picked up a local paper and saw that Gorman Gillett had passed away."

"And you knew then that if something happened to Frankline Gillett, your brother's secret would be safe?"

"That was not it at all," the witness said. "Gillett used that bereavement to make new demands on us. I learned of them over the telephone. He wanted me to do something I couldn't do. I didn't kill him, and my brother didn't kill him, I'm sure of that."

"Tell us what you know about the new demands," Mason said.

Baxter said, "I telephoned my brother. He said I must come home in such a way as to make it appear I was still in Bakersfield. He said he couldn't explain but everything depended on it. I registered at a motel in Bakersfield. I said that I would have dinner and go to bed at an early hour. I had dinner, signed for it, went into the motel, rumpled up my bed, jumped in my car and drove at once to my estate. I arrived there shortly after eleven o'clock.

"I found Frankline Gillett there with my brother. Gillett wanted an absolutely unreasonable sum for what he called a final pay-off. He pointed out that since his father had died he was in a position to give us a final clearance. His argument was that while his father was alive someone might get his father to make some statement, or that the father might inadvertently betray us. The argument didn't seem too logical to me, although the father's death did undoubtedly cut down the chances of our discovery.

"Frankline told us he was in serious trouble, that he was going to have to silence the lips of a nosy female who had been spying on him, and that he was not only going to need money, he was going to need my support; that I was going to have to give him an alibi."

"And what happened?" Mason asked.

"I refused," Baxter said. "I told them that they could count me out. I would pay money, but I was not going to go on the witness stand and perjure myself to give Frankline Gillett an alibi in a murder case."

"Do you know anything about the plans he had?" Mason asked.

"He mentioned that he might have to leave the country. Frankly, I doubt that his plans were really definite, but he wanted a hundred thousand dollars in cash, and he wanted an alibi. We had a rather large sum of cash available, but I flatly refused to furnish an alibi for him. He said he had to find out just how much this nosy female had already told some lawyer about him and that he either had to keep her

172

from keeping an appointment the next morning or else be out of the country. He was in a very nervous state. At times his thinking didn't seem logical—well thought out. I was afraid he was cracking up."

"And then what happened?" Mason asked.

"I don't know," Baxter said. "He told us he had to find out just how bad a certain situation was, and that he'd be back about one o'clock in the morning. Then he went to his car."

"Where was his car?"

"He had parked his car down by the swimming pool. After my refusal, he left the house and walked toward the swimming pool.

"My brother and I were discussing the matter when we heard either the sound of a car backfiring or a shot. We ran out of the house but saw nothing. We looked around the grounds, saw nothing and heard nothing. We then heard a car driving out of the gates and we assumed that was Frankline Gillett leaving. We thought his car had backfired."

"What time was that?"

"That was just a few minutes before midnight."

"The gates were open?"

"The gates had been closed at ten o'clock, but my brother had opened them when Frankline Gillett called and stated he was coming out to discuss an important matter."

"Did Frankline Gillett tell you that he intended to commit a murder?"

"Yes. He didn't say who the victim was but he said he expected to be mixed up in a murder and that it was absolutely essential that he have an alibi the police would never question. He wanted me to furnish that alibi. He knew that I was supposed to have been in Bakersfield. He wanted me to swear that he had learned my location, that he had a business deal we were discussing, that he had driven to Bakersfield, and that we had been together in the motel ever since eleven o'clock in the evening.

"I am sorry this has come about. I am sorry the mask has been ripped from my brother's masquerade. I would have done anything to have avoided it, but one cannot argue with fingerprints. I have previously pointed out to him that the mistakes he made must eventually be paid for."

"I think," Perry Mason said, "that is all. I have no further questions. Does the district attorney care to cross-examine?"

Hamilton Burger frowned, turned to Nelson for a brief whipered conference, looked helplessly at Judge Laporte and said, "No questions."

"Now then," Perry Mason said, "I desire to recall one of the prosecutions's witnesses for further cross-examination."

"Who is the witness?" Judge Laporte asked.

"Nell Arlington," Mason said.

"If the Court please," Hamilton Burger said, "at this time we withdraw our objection. As we see it, the duty of our office is to vigorously prosecute persons accused of crime. But when it begins to appear that there are other matters involved, we are mindful of the fact that our primary duty is to see that justice is done."

Judge Laporte nodded and said. "Thank you for that statement, Mr. District Attorney. I think it exemplifies the principles of your office. Miss Arlington will come forward."

Nell Arlington arose reluctantly.

"You have already been sworn," Judge Laporte said, "just take the stand."

Nell Arlington walked to the witness stand.

Mason said. "You have testified that you acted sometimes as secretary for the defendant, that you opened the lists which she received giving the names of the prospects so that you could telephone the names and addresses to her if she called in?"

"Yes," the witness said crisply.

"And when those lists were telephoned in, you took them down and relayed the messages?"

"Yes."

"I noticed on this list which contains the name of Mrs. Frankline Gillett on 671 Tribly Way that there are eleven names on that list instead of ten, that the Tribly name is the last name on the list and that the typewriting is different from the typewriting in which the other ten names appear. I suggest to you, Miss Arlington, that you added that name to the list after the list had been received in the mail. Now, before you answer that question, remember that you're under oath, remember that the names that were on that list can be verified from the central bureau that sent them out, and remember that typewriting is as distinctive as handwriting and an expert on questioned documents can tell whether that name was written on your typewriter."

There was a long period of silence, then Nell Arlington said, "Very well, I wrote it."

"And the reason you wrote it," Mason said, "was because you had become suspicious. You wanted to know who was living at that address."

She said, "Looking through the things of the man who I thought was my husband I had found a driving license made out in the name of Frankline Gillett at that address. The ages of the men, the physical descriptions, were exactly the same. I didn't know what to make of it. I didn't know whether he had an alias or what. I wanted to find out what was there, so I typed that name, knowing that my friend, Gwynn Elston, would make a call at that address and I could then pump her as to what was there without her realizing that I had any personal interest."

"But," Mason said, "something happened, something that caused you to change your plans?"

"Of course something happened," she said. "You know what it was. My husband, or the man I thought was my husband, found out that Gwynn was making a call at this other address, and, of course, assumed that Gwynn would find out about his bigamy and tell me. He determined to kill her in order to keep her from talking. He fixed up a drink of gin and tonic and added strychnine. I didn't realize this until after Gwynn had left the house and after he had left the house and I found the bottle of strychnine tablets where he had left it after removing it from the medicine chest. I had *thought* Gwynn poured the drink down the washbowl. At the time, I thought merely that my husband had made it too strong.

"When Gwynn returned that evening and had a gun with her, I felt that the time had come for a show down. I tried to make her tell me, but she wouldn't. I could see she was lying. I put barbiturates in Gwynn's milk toast and, when she was safely asleep, I took the gun and went out to find my husband."

"And how did you start looking for him?" Mason asked.

She said, "I had known for some time that he was making his living by getting contributions from George Belding Baxter. I didn't know the reason for those contributions, but I decided to find out. I drove to the Baxter estate. I took the gun that I had taken from under Gwynn's pillow after she went to sleep. I felt certain that somehow Mr. Baxter held the key to the mystery, and . . . well, I had an idea I would find my husband there."

"You found him there?"

"I drove up," she said, "just as my husband emerged from the house. I caught him, so to speak, red-handed."

"And?" Mason asked.

"He saw me. He wanted to know what I was doing there, and when I accused him . . . well, I knew then that he had planned to murder me. He tried to strangle me. I pulled the trigger of the gun. He fell back on the lawn. I simply drove my car around the circle, went out through the gates and returned home. I put the gun under Gwynn's pillow again."

Mason turned to Hamilton Burger with something of a bow. "I think," he said, "that concludes the defendant's case."

# Chapter 16

Mason, Della Street and Paul Drake sat in the lawyer's office conducting a post-mortem on the case.

Mason said, "Well, it shows the importance of fighting every step of the way. It also shows what a peculiar twist fate can sometimes give to a case.

"The housekeeper was telling the truth about having lost the gun. Frankline Gillett, returning to his residence on Tribly Way, after having completed a visit with his second wife on Mandala Drive, found the gun on the side of the road. It was a new gun and a nice gun, and no doubt he stopped his car, picked it up and took it home with him.

"By that simple act he involved George Belding Baxter in the case. Of course, at the time he had absolutely no idea where that gun had come from. To him it was simply manna from heaven, a gun lying by the side of the road. He picked it up and took it with him.

"Gillett had an absolutely foolproof method of blackmail. He needed only to tap the till any time he wanted anything. George Belding Baxter had been a real estate salesman when his brother got in trouble and escaped while he was en route to the penitentiary. An officer was murdered, but probably the brother is innocent of that and can clear himself. George changed his last name, took his brother with him as Corley L. Ketchum and they started in business together.

"Then Baxter became prosperous. They wanted to put his picture in the paper. Naturally, if his brother had been a partner, they would have wanted to put the brother's picture in the paper, and that would have led to complications. So the brother was forced into a position of insignificance. He had to live his entire life masquerading as a gardener and caretaker. There's a touch of poetic justice here. Gorman Gillett went to prison, paid his debt to society and was able to live his own life, even if it was rather a frugal life. But it was, nevertheless, an independent life.

"Collington Halsey had to live a life of deceit. He had to live in perpetual fear and the man's native abilities were forced to lie dormant under the masquerade he had to assume.

"And then both brothers had to pay blackmail.

"Eighteen months earlier Gillett had become infatuated with Nell Arlington. He was a little tired of his routine home life with his legitimate wife. So he committed bigamy and felt that as long as he didn't have to make a living at any particular business the chances of his being discovered were very negligible.

"Then, because he was away from home so much, Nell wanted her friend, Gwynn Elston, to come and live with her, and Gillett had to consent to that.

"Slowly, inexorably, the man became trapped within the web of his own chicanery. The fact that he was desperate is shown by the fact that he was willing to give Gwynn Elston strychnine in her drink, hoping that she would go into convulsions and die, and he and Nell could testify to enough facts to avoid an inquest.

"In other words, Gillett was one of a type; a man who doesn't think very far ahead but plots to escape from one predicament as fast as it develops without carefully planning the whole situation."

"All of which shows," Paul Drake said, "that a lawyer should always be loyal to his clients. But I don't think I'd ever have had the sheer guts to have stood up to a man of George Belding Baxter's influence, Perry."

"It's more than being loyal to your clients," Mason said thoughtfully. "It's being loyal to the basic principles of justice. And when you're trying to do that, you have to take it on the chin once in a while—or at least be ready to."

"Ready, able and willing, is the legal expression," Della Street said, and her eyes as she looked at Perry Mason showed the depth of her feeling.

# Attention Mystery and Suspense Fans

Do you want to complete your collection of mystery and suspense stories by some of your favorite authors? John D. MacDonald, Helen MacInnes, Dick Francis, Amanda Cross, Ruth Rendell, Alistar MacLean, Erle Stanley Gardner, Cornell Woolrich, among many others, are included in Ballantine/Fawcett's new Mystery Brochure.

For your FREE Mystery Brochure, fill in the coupon below and mail it to: